MONTANA MAVERICKS

Welcome to Big Sky Country! Where spirited men and women discover love on the range.

LEGACY OF TENACITY

As the town begins to heal from its scars and scandals, its single cowboys (and cowgirls) are ready for a fresh start. They know that love can grow in the most unexpected places and that down doesn't mean out. So make a wish on a Montana moon for all to be revealed—they've waited for their sweethearts long enough!

MAVERICK'S PRINCE CHARMING

Divorced dad Gideon Frost is devoted to his four-year-old son, Scotty, dedicated to his ranch and good at his job as an attorney. But that doesn't stop him from wanting more. He's been working with fun-loving, vivacious lawyer Lynda Slater for two years, and his crush on her has only gotten stronger. Lynda insists she's not interested in committing to anyone, but after their unexpectedly romantic encounter at a masquerade ball, Gideon suddenly has reason to hope...

Dear Reader,

Lynda Slater isn't looking for love, marriage or children. She'd sworn off those things years ago. Her mantra in life is to enjoy men but never take them seriously. As a divorce lawyer in the little town of Tenacity, Montana, she sees bitter, heartbroken spouses enter her office nearly every day. She doesn't want or need that kind of pain. And she doesn't see her opinion on love changing. That is, until Tenacity holds a fundraising masquerade ball. On the dance floor, something very mystical happens to Lynda when a knight in shining armor kisses her, then mysteriously disappears before she can learn his identity. Shaken by the encounter, she sets out on a mission to find him.

Gideon Frost has had a crush on Lynda ever since he'd taken a position at Fiske and Jones law firm. But being six years younger than her and a divorcé raising his four-year-old son, he knows he doesn't have a chance of catching beautiful Lynda's attention. And when, under his knight disguise, he kisses her at the ball, he isn't expecting his life to change in that moment. But suddenly he's wondering if he has a chance to make Lynda a part of his family. And what will she think if she learns he's her mysterious knight?

I hope you enjoy reading how Lynda learns about truly falling in love and how Gideon convinces her that when something is "written in the stars" it's meant to last forever.

Love and best wishes,

Stella Bagwell

MAVERICK'S PRINCE CHARMING

STELLA BAGWELL

MONTANA MAVERICKS

Special thanks and acknowledgment are given to Stella Bagwell for her contribution to the Montana Mavericks: Legacy of Tenacity miniseries.

Recycling programs for this product may not exist in your area.

ISBN-13: 978-1-335-54088-1

Maverick's Prince Charming

For questions and comments about the quality of this book, please contact us at CustomerService@Harlequin.com.

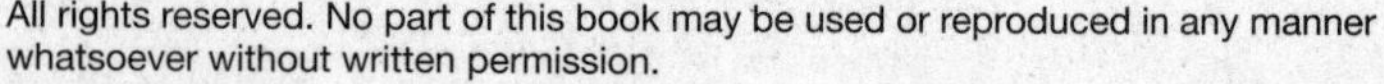

Harlequin Enterprises ULC
22 Adelaide St. West, 41st Floor
Toronto, Ontario M5H 4E3, Canada
www.Harlequin.com

HarperCollins Publishers
Macken House, 39/40 Mayor Street Upper,
Dublin 1, D01 C9W8, Ireland
www.HarperCollins.com

Printed in Lithuania

After writing more than one hundred books for Harlequin, **Stella Bagwell** still finds writing about two people discovering everlasting love very rewarding. She loves all things Western and has been married to her own real cowboy for fifty-four years. Living on the south Texas coast, she also enjoys being outdoors and helping her husband care for the animals on the small ranch they call home. The couple has one son, who teaches high school mathematics and coaches football and powerlifting.

Books by Stella Bagwell

Montana Mavericks: Legacy of Tenacity

Maverick's Prince Charming

The Fortunes of Texas: Fortune's Hidden Treasures

Fortune's Mr. Right

Harlequin Special Edition

Men of the West

Her Kind of Doctor
The Arizona Lawman
Her Man on Three Rivers Ranch
A Ranger for Christmas
His Texas Runaway
Home to Blue Stallion Ranch
The Rancher's Best Gift
Her Man Behind the Badge
His Forever Texas Rose
The Baby That Binds Them
Sleigh Ride with the Rancher
The Wrangler Rides Again
The Other Hollister Man
Rancher to the Rescue
The Cowboy's Road Trip

Visit the Author Profile page
at Harlequin.com for more titles.

To all you loyal Montana Mavericks readers,
thank you for loving this series as much as I do.

Chapter One

Lynda Slater swiped a coat of matte red lipstick over her lips, then stepped back from the large mirror in the busy powder room to give her appearance one final inspection. When she'd first donned the Cleopatra costume she'd chosen to wear for the Written in the Stars masquerade ball, she'd been smitten with the wide bejeweled golden collar that rested over the seafoam-green gown. The wispy chiffon flowed all the way to the floor and was cinched at the waist with a gem encrusted belt to match the collar. But now, in spite of the March night being cold, even for Tenacity, Montana, standards, she was on the verge of sweating. A result of dancing to nearly every song the band had played so far tonight.

A naughty little smile curved her red lips as she adjusted the golden ornate headdress perched over her long auburn hair. Maybe she should have gone with the skimpy French maid number, she thought. With very little fabric to the mini skirt, the garment would have certainly been cooler.

But Lynda already had the reputation of being a party girl with emphasis on *party*. And tonight she wanted the townspeople to be focused on donating to Tenacity's Dinosaur Center. Lucky weather and the will of the town had meant construction of the center had gone faster than anticipated—so fast they'd been able to host the ball here.

"Hey, Lynda. Nice ball, don't you think?"

Readjusting the green jeweled mask on her face, Lynda turned to see a young woman dressed as Cinderella. Because most of her face was covered with a white silky mask to match her Victorian wig, Lynda wasn't certain of the woman's identity, but she thought it was Rhonda, who worked at the one and only drug store in town.

"To be honest, I never thought it would turn out to be this much of a success. The band couldn't be better, and the crowd is huge. I just hope everyone is contributing whatever amount they can afford to the Dinosaur Center fund. Ka-ching, ka-ching!" she said with a laugh, then asked, "By the way, how do you know I'm Lynda?"

Cinderella made an imaginary hourglass shape with her hands. "Your curves aren't exactly disguised by that fabulous gown."

Lynda laughed. "I'll take that as a compliment."

"Trust me. It was given as one," Cinderella said as she walked out of the powder room.

Lynda took another moment to smooth a hand over her long hair before she made her way back to the ballroom, where the crowd on the dance floor appeared to be even thicker than when she left it only minutes ago.

The large conference room in the building was festively decorated with colorful streamers hanging from the ceiling, along with strings of lights. On one side of the room a long table with refreshments had been erected, while down the wall from it, another table was set up for guests to make their donations and also purchase trinkets to commemorate tonight's ball.

She was tapping her foot to the music and thinking she might walk over to the donation table to see how the contributions were going when a gravelly, unfamiliar voice spoke directly behind her.

"Very nice party, wouldn't you say?"

Turning, she was faintly surprised to see a man she'd never seen around town before. At least, from what she could see of his face behind his mask, she didn't think she recognized him. He was dressed as Captain Hook and ogling her as though she was bounty on a pirate ship.

Normally Lynda was friendly with everyone, even strangers. But something about this man's hard eyes sent up warning signals.

"Extremely nice," she said politely.

He stepped to her side. "Would you like to dance?"

She would like to dance but not necessarily with him, she thought. Still, this was a fundraising ball, and she didn't want to insult this man when he might possibly be contributing a hefty amount to the Dinosaur Center fund.

She plastered a fake smile on her face. "Sure," she said.

They walked onto the dance floor before he took her by the hand, and Lynda was somewhat relieved when he didn't pull her into a tight clench. Which was a surprising reaction from her, considering how much she normally enjoyed male attention.

"I'm new in town," he told her. "So I thought the ball would be a good place to meet people."

The fact that he wasn't a citizen of the Tenacity area hardly surprised Lynda. Most of the folks in and around her hometown were the warm-and-friendly sort. This guy had a cool vibe about him and not the kind that generated swagger.

"Hello, I'm Lynda," she said. "Planning on staying in Tenacity long?"

"I'm not sure. My stay depends on a few things."

Normally she would've invited him to explain. Being a lawyer for the past several years, she knew how to get information from a person, even when they were reluctant to give it. But in Captain Hook's case, she didn't want to give him the idea she was interested.

"Well, I hope your visit to Tenacity is enjoyable," she said politely. "We have a nice little town."

"And from what I understand, Tenacity is catching the attention from outsiders with this dinosaur dig you're planning."

As he moved her slowly around the dance floor, she wondered how much longer the song was going to last. It had already felt too long to her.

She said, "Everyone is hoping the dig will put Tenacity on the map. We need something to boost our economy around here, and the dig might provide a flow of added income."

"Could be. If you discover more dinosaur bones—or something else."

Thinking his remark was odd, she looked at him. But with little more than his eyes showing behind his pirate's mask, it was difficult to decipher his thoughts.

"What do you mean by 'something else'?" she asked.

"Precious metals? Like gold? I seriously doubt anything like that would be uncovered. I've never heard of any panning or mining being done in this area before."

In spite of the mask, she could see his eyes had narrowed. Creepy—that was the ambiance she was getting from the man.

He said, "Well, a person never knows what he'll find when he digs beneath the surface."

By the time the song ended and he released his hold on her, Lynda was more than relieved to walk away and lose herself in the crowd.

She was visiting the refreshment table when she spotted John Erickson, a coworker and single guy in his thirties, helping himself to a cup of punch. He was dressed like Daniel Boone, complete in buckskin clothing and a coonskin cap. His mask was small and barely covered his eyes, but she would've known him anyway. Although he was a young man, he detested exercise and loved food, and it showed around his waistline.

"Hi, John! Enjoying the ball so far?"

"This is amazing. Who would've thought we could have an event this size in Tenacity. I don't know about you, but it warms my heart."

"I couldn't be happier. Hopefully this is a sign of better times to come for our little town," she said as she gazed out at the sea of dancing couples, all of whom were dressed in costumes and masks. "I love the masquerade part of tonight. It's fun, even though I do recognize most of the people I'm acquainted with."

"Speaking of masquerade, who was the guy with

the hook? I've never seen the guy around before to-night," he said.

Lynda rolled her eyes toward the ceiling. "I have no idea. And I didn't ask him for a last name. He was just too creepy for my taste."

"Creepy? Why? Did he make a pass at you?"

Chuckling, she said, "He didn't. He was just—giving off weird vibes. Like he's here at the ball for some other reason besides dancing and socializing."

"Hmm. Perhaps he's here just to donate to the Dinosaur Center. But if that was the case, he didn't need to dress up and attend the event."

Nodding, Lynda said, "Right. Anyone could drop off a contribution at the center. But maybe I'm thinking all wrong about the guy. I hope so."

They talked for a few more minutes before John spotted a woman he wanted to dance with, and after quickly excusing himself, Lynda left the refreshment area. She was working her way to the area of the floor where the band was situated on an elevated stage when someone tapped her on the shoulder.

Hoping it wasn't weirdo Captain Hook wanting another dance, she turned and was pleasantly surprised to see a tall, ruggedly built man dressed as a knight in shining armor. Because his face was mostly covered with a silver mask to match his headgear and breastplate, she couldn't begin to guess his identity. She was just grateful it wasn't creepy Captain Hook.

Without saying a word, he indicated that he'd like to dance with her, and Lynda happily obliged by offering the man her hand.

Just as he escorted her onto the dance floor, the song came to an end, and while they waited for the next tune to begin, Lynda was highly aware of the snug hold the man had on her hand. She also noted there were calluses on his palm at the base of his fingers, which told her this man had some sort of manual job.

She was wondering about his occupation when the band began to play again. This time the tempo of the music wasn't quite as fast, but neither was it a barely-move-your-feet kind of song. Not that it mattered to Lynda. Actually, she didn't think it would be a bit repulsive to be crushed up in this knight's arms. From what she could see of his brown eyes, they were warm and inviting. His brows were hidden by the helmet he was wearing, but judging by the thick dark veil of lashes framing his eyes, she figured they were also dark and heavy enough to be expressive.

As he began to guide her across the dance floor, he pulled her slightly closer, and for one reckless second, Lynda considered resting her cheek against his shoulder. But she didn't know this man from Adam. And sure, she liked men a lot, but that didn't mean she went around playing up to strangers.

The guy was definitely light on his feet, she thought a moment later, and by far a much better dancer than creepy Captain Hook. He wasn't giving off weird vibes, either. In fact, the longer they danced, the more Lynda was experiencing pleasant little tingles rushing over her skin.

One thing for certain—he was definitely the quiet sort. Since he'd invited her to dance, he'd not uttered one word. Maybe that was because the two of them were strangers and he didn't know what to talk to her about, she thought.

He's a man and you're a woman, Lynda. That should be enough to strike up a conversation.

Silently agreeing with the daring little voice in her head, she opened her mouth to ask him his name but stopped herself at the last second. After all, this was a masquerade ball. Identities were supposed to be hidden. Besides, there wasn't any point in her ruining a perfectly nice dance with unnecessary words.

The same thought must have been running through his mind, Lynda decided. Without speaking a word, he suddenly tightened his hold on her hand and drew her closer. Not enough to cause the fronts of their bodies to touch, but certainly close enough for her nerves to coil with anticipation. She didn't know what was happening, but the longer they danced, the more she recognized a magical aura was building around them.

As the song reached a crescendo, Mr. Knight picked up the pace to match the tempo and then unexpectedly twirled her beneath his arm. She made the turn smoothly, but the inertia of making the full circle caused her to stumble slightly forward and straight into his arms.

"Oh! I'm so sorry!" she exclaimed.

He caught her effortlessly, and as his strong hands steadied her, she looked up at him. For an instant their gazes locked, and before Lynda could think or know what she was doing, she raised up on the tips of her toes and angled her mouth up to his.

The instant their lips touched, Lynda was transported to somewhere far away from the crowded dance floor.

Even the loud music became nothing but a dim background noise. The faint taste of mint and chocolate was on his lips, but it was the raw male flavor that was drawing her in, urging her to kiss him with a fervor that shocked even her.

She wasn't sure which one of them was the first to break the fiery contact. Whether it had been him or her hardly mattered. The kiss had been enough to shake Lynda all the way down to her toes and leave her knees so weak she marveled that she was still standing.

As her eyes continued to delve into the brown depth of his, a tangle of wild thoughts and feelings zipped through her. Questions formed on her tongue, but she was so rattled she could only manage to utter a few breathless words. "I don't even know who you are."

He opened his mouth to speak, but before he could say a word, his phone buzzed. Still dazed from the heated kiss they'd exchanged, she watched as he fished the phone from a pocket on his costume.

As soon as he spotted the ID of the caller, he swiped to answer, and seeing that he'd chosen to take the call rather than continue to dance, she figured he probably wanted his privacy and she should make a quiet exit.

But she didn't want to just turn and walk away. Not without his name.

"I'll be right there," he said. "Yeah. I'm leaving now."

Had she heard that voice before? It sounded so familiar. But with the loud music playing and his helmet muffling his words, she couldn't be sure of what she was hearing. The man ended the call, and as he slipped the phone back into his pocket, he glanced at her. "Sorry. I have to leave," he said. "Thanks for the dance."

Too stunned by their brief but mind-blowing encounter to make a reply, Lynda watched him stride away until he'd disappeared in the crowd of dancers. Only then did she realized he'd dropped something when he'd turned to go, and she quickly bent down to collect the small object.

The key chain with a small plastic tyrannosaurus rex attached to it was one of the commemorative trinkets being sold at the ball tonight, and after turning it over in her hand, she was disappointed to see there was no name or phone number attached.

Oh well, she thought. Surely it wouldn't be that hard to find one shining knight in the little town of Tenacity. But even if she was lucky enough to find him, would she have another chance to kiss him? She could only hope.

The next morning, at his parent's house on Pine Ridge Ranch, Gideon Frost sat at the kitchen table, hurriedly downing a cup of black coffee.

"Mom, are you sure I don't need to take Scotty into town to see his pediatrician? I'll call the office and tell them I have to take off today," he said to his mother.

Joanne Frost was a very young fifty-two, with light brown hair usually worn in a braid down her back. Gideon's father, Ash, often said he'd be in the gutter if it hadn't been for Joanne, and down through the years, they'd worked as a team to make sure the ranch remained profitable. Theirs was the kind of genuine and solid marriage Gideon had wanted for himself. Instead, at age twenty-seven, he'd already been divorced for a few years.

Not bothering to glance around at her son, Joanne calmly continued to wash a sink full of early breakfast dishes.

"There's no need for that," she told Gideon. "Scotty's temperature is perfectly fine this morning, and he appears to be feeling okay. Keeping him home from preschool is enough precaution."

Normally after a half day at preschool, Scotty spent the remainder of the day at a childcare center until Gideon got off work at five. But with the boy spiking a fever last night, he thought it best to have his grandmother watching over him.

"The fever could come back, Mom," Gideon said worriedly. "He could be coming down with a virus."

"Yes, and he could have simply played too hard yesterday," Joanne reasoned. "Kids can run a fever for what seems like no reason. Then a few hours later they're up and playing like nothing ever happened. I expect Scotty will be fine. I'll keep a close eye on him. No need for you to worry."

"All right, Mom. If you say so." Leaving his seat at the table, he carried his empty cup over to the sink and dropped it into the sudsy water. "And thanks for your help today. I hope you didn't have anything important planned."

She directed an affectionate wink at him. "What's more important than my grandchild's health? I can't think of anything."

He chuckled. "Maybe the health of your husband and son. We might be important, too."

With a light laugh, she gave him a one-armed hug

around the back of his waist. "Well, I suppose you two are also high on my list."

"See you later, Mom. Call me if you need me." He pecked a light kiss onto her cheek before turning and starting out of the room. "I'll go through the living room on my way out and tell Scotty goodbye."

When he entered the simple but comfortably furnished living room, he found his four-year-old son sitting cross-legged on the couch. He was still wearing his footed pajamas and the sock cap Gideon had pulled over his ears before they'd left his house early this morning. Relatives and friends all said that Scotty resembled Gideon. The boy was tall for his age and he did have dark hair and eyes like Gideon's, but otherwise he thought he faintly resembled his mother, Cecily. Or maybe that was because little Scotty had been one of the initial reasons his ex-wife had wanted a divorce. Becoming pregnant on their wedding night, adjusting to married life, and being a young mother had been too much for her.

"Hey, Dad, I nearly have this whole page colored all ready. It looks good, don't it?" he asked as he looked eagerly up at his father.

"Doesn't it?" Gideon corrected his son, then peered closer at the coloring book lying on Scotty's lap. "Hmm. I don't see one place where you've gotten out of the lines. Good work."

"Aw, Dad, I haven't gotten out of the lines since I was three, and that was a long time ago."

Smiling, he ruffled the top of Scotty's head. "Mind your grandmother, and I'll see you this evening, buddy."

Scotty grinned up at him. "I'll be good, Dad. Bye."

Gideon left the house, and as he climbed into his truck, he tried to push away the guilty pangs he'd been having ever since he'd hurried away from the masquerade ball last night. While he'd been out dancing and kissing his coworker, his son had spiked a fever. He should've been home with his child instead of pursuing a woman who didn't know he existed. At least not in a romantic sense.

She'd certainly kissed you like you existed, Gideon. A few more seconds of the kind of lip-lock she placed on you and you might have wilted right there on the dance floor.

Shoving at the embarrassing voice going off in his head, Gideon steered the truck away from his parents' house and headed it down a narrow graveled lane that would eventually take him to a junction of the main highway leading into town.

On either side of the road, pasture land of low rolling hills spread to distant mountain ridges, but this morning Gideon wasn't seeing the brown grassy slopes or the Black Angus cattle foraging among the clumps of sage. Instead, he was seeing Lynda—her silky auburn hair flowing down the back of her green dress, her red lips parted temptingly.

Damn it, he needed to stop thinking about that damned kiss. Frankly, he didn't know what had prompted him to ask Lynda to dance with him in the first place. She'd been the belle of the ball and had danced with nearly every guy in the room. He'd been foolish to think he might make an impression on her with his shiny knight-in-armor suit. She had men trying to impress her every day of the week. What was one more to her, he thought dully.

In the town of Tenacity, he drove straight to the law offices of Fiske and Jones, where he'd worked for the past two and a half years since he'd earned his law degree. Lynda, being six years older than Gideon, had worked for the firm much longer. She was a dynamo in the courtroom, and there wasn't a person on staff who didn't envy her looks and brains and free-spirit attitude about life. In spite of his better judgment, Gideon had crushed on her ever since he'd laid eyes on the woman. And now that the two of them worked in the same firm, the crush had grown even deeper.

Carrying the briefcase filled with work he'd sat up late to finish last night, he entered the building through a back door. As he made his way down a narrow hallway to his office, he heard a mix of voices coming from the break room, along with Lynda's rich laughter.

No one else laughed like Lynda. The vivacious sound made him want to think everything was right with the world, even if storm clouds were brewing in the near distance.

A quick glance at his wristwatch told him it wasn't quite yet time for the doors to the law firm to open and for the staff to get to work.

"Hey, Gideon, come have some coffee," John Erickson called to him. "There's still plenty in the pot. And Mary brought apple fritters this morning. They'll be gone soon if you don't get one now."

Gideon walked on into the room and came to stand next to the paralegal. "Thanks, John," Gideon told him. "But I've already had breakfast."

Mary Pernell, a secretary in her sixties, pulled a playful face at Gideon, then patted her hip. "I know. You make a point of eating healthy, while my diet is worse than criminal. But it's okay to be decadent once in a while, Gideon. It hasn't killed me yet."

Actually the secretary, who'd been divorced for several years, appeared young for her age. With her salt-and-pepper hair cut into a smooth bob and her face wearing only a few wrinkles, she could pass for ten years younger.

"Trust me, Mary, I was decadent this morning. I ate Mom's biscuits and gravy," he told her, then turned his attention to Lynda. Her perfectly manicured fingers were twiddling with a tyrannosaurus rex key chain, just like the ones being sold at the masquerade ball last night. He'd purchased one to give to Scotty as a souvenir. However this morning, when he'd boxed up the knight suit in preparation to return it to the costume rental, he'd searched through the pockets for the key chain, but it had been missing.

"Good morning, Gideon," Lynda said with a bright smile for him. "We were just talking about the marvelous party you and Mary missed last night."

Mary chuckled. "It was easier for me to donate my money through a check. After the day I had yesterday, the only thing I wanted to do last night was flop onto the couch in front of the TV. But my quiet time didn't last long. My granddaughters were ripping through the house like it was a speedway."

Recently, Fay, one of Mary's three grown daughters, who was also divorced, had moved back in with her mother and brought her two daughters, ages six and four, with her. It was obvious that Mary loved her daughter and granddaughters and wanted to help them, but Gideon could also see how the housing situation had interrupted the woman's quiet life.

"I understand, Mary. Sometimes Scotty runs through the house like he's in the Kentucky Derby. That's when he gets a time-out. Which he hates."

She looked at Gideon. "Uh, by the way, how is Scotty this morning?"

Gideon didn't miss the look of concern Lynda gave the woman before she turned the same expression on him. Did she really care if Scotty had been ill? He'd heard her say more than once that kids weren't her thing.

"Is something wrong with your little boy?" Lynda asked.

Shaking his head, he said, "He spiked a fever last night. But he seems fine this morning. I've kept him home from preschool, and my mom is watching him." He glanced over to Mary. "How did you know Scotty was ill?"

"You mother and I have a mutual friend," Mary explained. "She said she talked to Joanne last night, and it was obvious to her that your mother was worried about her grandson. I'm glad to hear Scotty's better this morning. There's nothing more worrisome than a sick child."

"Mom will keep a close eye on him," Gideon said.

After a moment, Lynda said, "Well, it's a shame you missed the party, Gideon. When I left the Dinosaur Center some of the committee members were still counting money. Everyone connected to the event seems to be happy with the outcome."

John chuckled slyly. "I don't know about the donations, but I'm sure happy about the telephone numbers I picked up from several ladies last night. Who would have thought a Daniel Boone costume would have attracted the women?"

Mary rolled her eyes. "Now John has a big problem," she said to Gideon. "He doesn't know which woman to call first."

"A great problem to have, right, Gideon?" John joked.

Gideon did his best to chuckle, even though his mind was only taking in a portion of the conversation going on between his coworkers. During the twenty-minute drive into town this morning, he'd been rehearsing a reason to give Lynda for that kiss he'd given her. Or that she'd given him. Hell, their lip-lock had been so intense, he couldn't be sure who'd initiated the kiss—or ended it. Either way, he'd expected Lynda to light into him about it as soon as he'd walked into the building this morning. But so far she was looking at him as though nothing had happened between the two of them. Had she truly not recognized him?

He poured himself a half cup of coffee and sat down in the empty chair to her right. What was he going to do? he wondered. Ask her outright? Forget the kiss ever happened? Damn it, had he turned into a complete fool?

"What I'm wondering is if anyone at the ball last night recognized the Captain Hook guy," John asked. "Lynda, did you find out who he was?"

As she shook her head Gideon noticed she looked as fresh and vibrant as if she'd had ten hours of sleep instead of dancing half the night away. But then, he supposed Lynda was accustomed to late hours. She was often talking about her social life keeping her out until the wee hours of the morning. Why the heck Gideon had a crush on the woman was a question he wished he could answer. Maybe then he could do something about getting her completely out of his system.

She said, "I asked around, but no one seemed to know him. You can be certain of one thing though—he was the epitome of creepiness."

Captain Hook? Right before Gideon had walked into the ballroom, he'd spotted Lynda dancing with a guy in a pirate's costume. Earlier, he'd noticed the man working his way through the crowd and as he'd watched him approaching one woman after another, Gideon had sensed the guy was a creep. Which had given him an extra good reason to ask Lynda to dance with him. As long as he'd held her in his arms on the dance floor, Captain Hook couldn't press her to dance with him again.

Gideon asked, "What do you mean?"

Frowning, she said, "He made my skin crawl. Something about his eyes. He looked like the accused at the defense table when everyone—including his lawyer—knows he's guilty."

"Did he talk? Say lewd things to you?" Gideon pressed her.

"He talked. But none of what he said was actually offensive. There was just something off about his comments. He'd heard about the dinosaur dig and seemed to be quite interested in it."

Mary said, "Well, I don't see anything unusual about that. The town of Tenacity has been trying to get the word out about the dinosaur dig. We want outsiders to get interested and bring in much needed money to our businesses. And the masquerade ball was all about promoting the dig as well as the center."

"True," Lynda replied. "But this man's interest seemed... different. He even hinted that a dig might unearth something far more valuable than dinosaur bones."

"Like what?" Gideon asked, while thinking he disliked the man, even though he'd not had any contact with him. If he gave Lynda the creeps, that was enough to convince Gideon the guy was not exactly a model character.

"I asked him if he was implying there might be precious metals like gold or silver in the area. But he didn't answer my question. To be honest, he seemed rather evasive."

"I imagine the guy was just trying to catch your attention or impress you with the idea that he was some sort of mining engineer or something," John said. "Don't you figure he was harmless?"

"Probably. I'm going to put Captain Hook out of my mind," she said, and then a dreamy smile crossed her face. "But I'm not about to forget the knight in shining armor."

Mary's brows peeked with interest. "Who was he? One of your many boyfriends in disguise?"

Lynda's laugh was low and vibrant, making Gideon wonder just exactly what she was thinking about the knight she'd apparently not recognized.

"No. Believe me, if he'd been a guy I've dated, I would've recognized him," Lynda said. "No, this man was all new to me."

Gideon very nearly spewed the coffee in his mouth across the table and over his coworkers. How could she not have guessed his identity? She saw him every day here at the office. The two of them talked frequently throughout the day. But then, he supposed she'd never taken the time to really notice him as a man. She was too busy thinking of him as a dad with a little kid.

"So what was so special about Mr. Knight? Was he good looking?" Mary asked.

"Very. At least, what I could see of him beneath his helmet and mask. We danced, and before the song was completely over, he got a call and had to leave in a hurry. I didn't get his name or where he lived. Now I have no idea how to find him."

Gideon didn't know whether to feel elated or worried. One thing he did know—now would not be a good time to confess he was her knight in shining armor. No, he'd best keep that little secret to himself. Not that he enjoyed being a bit deceitful. Actually, Gideon hated being dishonest for any rhyme or reason. His ex-wife had deserved an Academy Award for her ability to tell convincing lies. For far too long, he'd believed her nights out on the town had been innocent evenings spent with girlfriends. Instead, those nights he'd been walking the floor with a crying, colicky baby, she'd been seeing other men.

No, Gideon didn't want any more deceit in his life. But he didn't want Lynda upset with him, either.

Awkwardly clearing his throat, he asked, "Uh, why would you want to find him? You just had one dance together."

Her dark auburn brows pulled together as she frowned at him. "How do you know we only had one dance together?"

Resisting the urge to clear his throat again, he took a swig of coffee, then attempted to answer. "Do you always have to cross-examine people?"

She rolled her pretty blue eyes as though she considered his question boring. How bored would she be if he suddenly confessed that he was Mr. Knight? Gideon wondered.

"In case you haven't noticed, I'm a lawyer. It's my job to inquire," she explained with exaggerated patience.

"But I'm not a witness," he replied. "And you said *danced.* I assumed that meant one song."

She blew out a breath as though she was almost embarrassed to admit it was only one dance. And as though she considered him something special. Oh Lord, this whole thing was becoming ridiculous.

"Okay. I'll admit I only danced one time with Mr. Knight. But we, uh, we shared a moment that, well, was frankly earth shaking."

Earth shaking? Yeah! She'd finally gotten something right, Gideon thought. The memory of that kiss she'd planted onto his lips was still enough to make his insides sizzle.

Mary let out a gasp of surprise, while John leaned eagerly forward.

"Lynda! Exactly what kind of moment are you talking about?" Mary quickly asked.

Gideon couldn't help but notice a pink swathe of color sweeping across her cheeks. Which was surprising in itself. He'd known Lynda for over two years, and during that time he'd rarely spotted a blush on her face.

"Well, we, uh… It was one of those meet-me-under-the-mistletoe kind of moments," she said cleverly.

John chuckled wickedly. "Only Christmas has come and gone, Lynda. In case you didn't notice, those were paper streamers hanging from the ceiling. Not clumps of mistletoe."

Lynda groaned. "Okay. Maybe I am being silly. But I— Something happened between us, and I need to find him. To see if it was just a…reaction to the festive evening."

Something *had* happened, Gideon thought. The kiss they'd shared had knocked him for a loop. So much so that he'd hardly recognized his phone had been ringing. And then when he'd seen it was his mother calling, he'd had to try to instantly shake himself back to reality.

Gideon was thinking about the way her soft lips had felt crushed beneath his when she suddenly held up the key chain with the little dinosaur dangling from the ring. Lynda was clutching the thing like the prince must have held on to Cinderella's lost slipper.

"This is all I have to go on," she said. "The man dropped this key chain when he turned to go. But there's no name or anything on it to give me a clue to his identity."

Mary said, "I wouldn't fret, Lynda. If it's meant for you to meet the guy again, you will."

"And if the, uh, moment you two had was actually that big of a deal, then I imagine the guy will be searching for you," John added with a sly grin.

Rising to her feet, Lynda dropped the key chain into the pocket of the waist-length velour jacket she was wearing over a wrap dress. From the very first day Gideon had come to work at Fiske and Jones, he'd instantly noticed Lynda Slater was a bombshell. With her long auburn hair, sultry blue eyes, provocative smiles, and shapely figure, she was the sort of woman a man's dreams were made of. And in those early days, he'd expected to walk into the office building and see her dressed in something risqué. But in the years since, he'd not once seen her wear anything to work that was overly revealing or out of place. Her appearance was completely professional both in the office and the courtroom, and he admired her for that. As for her free rein about going after any unattached man that caught her eye, he couldn't be as condoning as Mary seemed to be.

Mary seemed to admire Lynda for being able to have a physical relationship with a man and keep her emotions totally detached. She often said if more women could be like Lynda there would be far fewer broken hearts.

Maybe the woman was right, Gideon thought. But what did a person get out of a purely sexual relationship? Other than physical pleasure? As far as he was concerned he couldn't live with such loose boundaries. Nor did he want Scotty to grow up with that reckless attitude about women. If the heart wasn't involved, then that made everything else mechanical.

Glancing at the watch on her wrist, Lydia remarked, "It's time someone opened the front door before our bosses get here."

"I'll deal with the doors," John offered and started out of the room.

Mary quickly followed him out of the break room, but Gideon hesitated to join their departure as Lynda stood there staring thoughtfully off in space.

"Are you okay?" he asked gently.

His voice seemed to draw her back to the present, and she glanced hopelessly up at him. "I'm okay. Just feeling like a bit of a fool," she said. Then, reaching over, she touched a hand to his forearm. "I'm sorry your son was ill last night. Is that the reason you didn't come to the ball? Yesterday you said you'd be there, but I never saw you."

Unable to look her directly in the eye, he glanced over at the cabinet holding the coffee machine. "I was planning on being there. But then Scotty—well, I needed to make sure he wasn't coming down with something serious. But it sounds like the ball was a big hit—even without me."

She smiled. "You're a dedicated father, Gideon. You should feel good about that."

"Being a parent takes priority with me. But you already knew that, didn't you?"

Nodding, she dropped her hand from his arm, and Gideon figured she didn't have the slightest clue as to how much her touch affected him. And he had no plans to ever let her know how attracted he was to her. To Lynda he'd be just another name to her long list of admirers.

"Since the first day you came to work here at Fiske and Jones I've known how important being a father is to you. At that time your little boy couldn't have been very old, and I remember you were worried about leaving him at daycare."

Surprised that she'd remembered that much about him, he said, "Scotty wasn't yet two years old back then, and my mother had been the only babysitter he'd had. But she was needing to help Dad on the ranch, and frankly, it was time I quit relying on her for childcare. You're right though—I was anxious about him that day." In retrospect, he shouldn't have been. Scotty had adjusted well, and Little Cowpokes Daycare Center had been the perfect place for his son.

"It's good you considered your mother's need for a break," she said. "Believe me, I've done my share of babysitting my nieces and nephews. Between my two sisters, they have six kids, and sometimes I felt like I was the mother."

He frowned. "You make it sound like a drudgery."

She let out a short laugh as she started toward the door. "Don't get me wrong, Gideon. I love my nieces and nephews, but mixing gallons of formula and changing a mountain of diapers isn't exactly my idea of entertainment. My calling is the courtroom. Not the nursery."

If he hadn't already known that he and Lynda were complete opposites, he should certainly know it now. In spite of his failed marriage and raising a baby basically on his own, he supposed plenty of men would shy away from the notion of being a husband and father. But Gideon believed there was something better waiting for him and Scotty. He believed with the right woman, he could have a happy family like his parents had enjoyed for close to thirty years.

Smiling faintly, he shrugged. "Everyone has their own idea of fun."

"Well, I hope you find what tickles your fancy." She gave him a saucy wink. "You deserve some fun, too, Gideon."

She swished on out the door, and for a long moment, Gideon stood there staring at the empty doorway.

Last night Lynda had been the belle of the ball. He'd stood on the fringes of the crowd, watching while she'd danced with one man after another. Then the creepy Captain Hook had claimed a dance with her and after the guy had guided her a short distance across the floor, Lynda's posture had grown stiff and uncomfortable. At that point, Gideon had felt driven to step in and rescue her. But he'd never expected their dance to end in an explosive kiss or for her to consider him to be her mystery dream man.

Snap out of it, Gideon! She's not thinking of you as her hot kissing partner. The knight in shining armor is the man on her mind.

And there was no way Gideon could reveal to her that he and the knight were one and the same. Not if he planned on keeping her friendship.

Chapter Two

By the time Lynda left the law office and headed to her little rented house on the north side of town, she wanted to banish the word *divorce* from her mind. She couldn't count how many times she'd read or heard the word since she'd sat down at her desk this morning.

You're a lawyer who specializes in divorces, Lynda. What the heck do you expect to hear and see at your desk? Crime reports? Rap sheets? Arrest records? Would that be more pleasant?

The taunting voice in her head put a twisted slant to her lips. What was she thinking? There were times the breakup of a marriage ultimately ended up causing crimes and arrests. And there were plenty of times she felt it was a good thing to see a woman send a controlling man packing, or vice versa. It was just a sad fact that some couples who'd believed they were deliriously in love weren't really in love at all. They'd simply been deluding themselves, and once the delusion wore off, reality was too much to bear.

Lynda, you need to go home and pour yourself a stiff drink. This disenchanted attitude of yours is not your style. Where is the fun-loving woman who knows bet-

ter than to let herself think about love and marriage and babies?

I'm right here, thinking about my knight, Lynda mentally shouted at the nagging voice in her head. She had to find the man and discover for herself whether the electricity of their kiss had been real or merely the mystical effect of the masquerade ball. Otherwise she didn't think she'd ever get the man out of her mind.

As she continued driving down the residential street toward home, Lynda almost turned onto a side street that would take her by the house her parents, Kitty and Walter, had purchased shortly after they'd married forty years ago. Lynda and her two sisters, Vanessa and Darcy, had lived there from the time they were born until all three had grown up and moved out on their own. The couple had called it home until five years ago. At that time, the economy had gotten so bad in Tenacity, many businesses around town were having trouble staying afloat. Her father's housing construction business, which for many years had done a booming business, had slowly grinded to a halt. And unable to make ends meet, even with her mother's teacher's salary, the Slaters had been forced to sell their home and move to Whitehorn.

Seeing her parents give up the home they'd cherished had broken the hearts of the entire Slater family. But of the three sisters, Lynda's hurt had been the deepest. With Darcy and Vanessa having families of their own, they didn't need to go to their parent's house where they'd grown up surrounded by love and security. Living alone had made the situation different for Lynda.

When she'd felt the need for home and family, she'd gone to her parents and the house she'd grown up in. Now strangers resided there with a junked car taking up most of the front yard, the paint beginning to peel on the clapboard siding, and a piece of plywood nailed over a broken window.

If her father saw the place, he'd mutter a few curse words, for sure. And her mother would simply cry. But in any case, Lynda was happy her parents were financially okay now and didn't have to worry about making ends meet.

No. Lynda didn't need to see the old home place this evening, she thought. Nor did she need a reminder that nothing stayed the same. She'd learned that lesson in her law-school days when she'd fallen hard for a med student. Good looking and charming, Perry had made her innocent young heart believe every promise he had made about loving her until the end of time, about wanting marriage and a family with her. But after a few months of sharing her bed with him, he'd turned his attention to another woman. Oh, he'd had the decency to tell her how much he'd enjoyed their time together, but according to him, all good things had to come to an end.

Funny how she could still remember the cold wash of reality pouring over her as she'd watched him walk out the door. At that moment the tender parts of her heart had frozen and she'd sworn to never allow another man to touch her emotions or use her for his own pleasure. The humiliating ordeal with Perry had changed her whole outlook on life and what it meant to be a woman. From then on, she'd begun to live her life the way she wanted. Free and easy with no commitments or chance of heartbreak. And she'd never once regretted her decision to put her own desires over that of a sexy, good-looking man.

When she reached her house, she pulled her little sedan beneath the carport attached to the left side of the house and entered the kitchen through a side door. Since she'd turned down the thermostat when she'd left for work this morning to save on heating cost, the rooms were a bit chilly, and she quickly walked to the hallway and adjusted the temperature on the furnace before she started peeling off her dress and ankle-strap high heels.

She'd managed to pull on a pair of cozy lounge pants and top when she heard her phone ringing from where she'd left it on the countertop in the kitchen.

Pulling her hair into a scrunchie, she went to the combination kitchen/dining area. By most standards, the house was small, but it was somewhat roomier than the apartment located on the opposite side of town where she'd been living for several years. She enjoyed this quieter area and the fact that neighbors weren't able to listen to her conversations through the walls. Especially when she had male company. However it was sad to know the house had become available because the couple who'd lived here had been forced to move away to find better jobs.

The phone went quiet before Lynda could reach it, but seeing the caller was her older sister, Vanessa, she promptly redialed her number.

"Hey, sis! Did I catch you at a bad time?" Vanessa asked cheerfully.

"No. I was changing clothes. I've only been home about ten minutes."

"You must have worked late this evening," she said.

Lynda sighed. "A little. I have court tomorrow, and I wanted to make sure I had every *i* dotted and *t* crossed. The man I'm representing deserves to keep what is rightfully his, not hand it over to a greedy gold-digger."

"Oh my. This is a surprise. You siding with the husband."

With her free hand, Lynda began to put a clean filter into the basket of the coffee maker and fill it with several scoops of coffee grounds.

"You have me all wrong, Van. I'm on the side of justice. Male or female, I want to make sure no one is cheated or taken advantage of just because the love has gone out of the marriage."

Vanessa made a mocking grunt. "I'm surprised you admit there was any love in the first place."

"I seriously doubt there was love. Not the genuine kind. But I wasn't going to say so. I know you already think I'm cold-hearted. I didn't want to worsen your opinion of me."

Vanessa chuckled. "Like that is going to change my mind about my middle sister? You've been cynical for years now. And that job of yours doesn't help matters."

"My job makes me a nice living. And here in Tenacity, having a job that makes a person a decent living nowadays is as scarce as hen's teeth."

Sighing, Vanessa said, "Yes, you said a mouthful there. So give me some good news. I was calling to see how the masquerade ball turned out. In case you're wondering if I was there and you missed seeing me behind my mask, you didn't. I couldn't find a sitter for my four kids. Everyone was going to the ball."

"Even Darcy? You two should have flipped a coin and the loser babysat for the other."

"Nice idea. But it wouldn't work. Bart came home from work with a stomach virus. She had to take care of him, plus her two little ones."

At thirty-six, Vanessa was the eldest of the sisters and had been married to Gage Richards for fifteen years. With three boys—Bailey, age twelve; Ian, age ten; Cameron just turned eight—and six-year-old girl, Martha, Vanessa had her hands full just keeping the kids fed and dressed and at school on time. And that didn't count her full-time job at the bank in the bookkeeping department.

Lynda liked to think of herself as a dynamo, but she wasn't sure she could keep up with Van's schedule. As for Darcy, she was also on the constant go with two daughters, seven-year-old Roseann and five-year-old Garland. She worked as a teacher's aide at the local elementary school, while her husband, Bart, worked as a technician for a satellite Wi-Fi service.

"Oh, so neither of my sisters were there. What a bummer for both of you. The ball was fantastic. The music was great, and the place was overflowing with people. And the costumes were so fun," Lynda told her.

"And what was your costume? When we last talked about the ball, I forgot to ask."

"I went as Cleopatra," Lynda said as she poured water into the coffee maker and closed the lid.

Vanessa's low laugh was suggestive. "I'll bet that was a sight. Did you wear a black wig? I don't believe Cleo was a redhead."

"No. My hair's too long to try to stuff up beneath a wig. And anyway, the headpiece had emeralds and rubies in it that sort of went with my hair color." She described the rest of the outfit.

"Sounds beautiful. Where did you find it? I wouldn't have thought the little costume shop here in town had anything like that to rent."

"I ordered it online. Actually, I went ahead and bought the thing. The shipping back was going to cost almost as much as the costume, so I thought what the heck. Maybe you or Darcy can wear it next year."

"Hah! Me in a Cleopatra outfit? Remember, sis, I've had four kids. I'm not exactly shaped like you. Not that I ever was."

"What are you talking about? You look great."

"Thanks, Lynda, but a woman has to know her limitations."

Chuckling, Lynda fetched a cup from the cabinet and filled it with the strong coffee. "So back to the ball—I do have good news," she informed her sister. "So far the donations have been more than I expected. I don't know where people are finding the money to give, but it's lifting my spirits to see the citizens are being as generous as they can be."

"Listen, the people of Tenacity have always been good, generous folks, and we all want to see the town do better. If the dinosaur dig and the center can bring in tourists who'll hopefully spend money while they're in town, then I say yippee."

Lynda eased into one of two chairs at a small pine table in the kitchen. "You know, sometimes I have nightmares about Tenacity becoming a ghost town. I dream I'm running down empty streets but no one is around. The stores are all shuttered, and tumbleweeds are blowing down Central Avenue. It's spooky."

"Honey, you've been watching too many old westerns. You know, the kind where the old mining town has been deserted except for some old hermit hiding out in the saloon. And then the slick, gunfighting hero rides in and everything comes to life."

"Hah! No. I've not been watching old westerns. Frankly, I've not watched any movies lately. I've had a few dates and extra work to keep me occupied."

"So what about last night? Did you do lots of dancing?" Vanessa asked slyly.

"Nearly every dance."

"And you didn't find Mr. Perfect? When is that ever going to happen, Lynda? You're thirty-three!"

"You make it sound like I'm getting long in the tooth!" Lynda retorted. "Am I beginning to show my age or something?"

"No. You're wasting time. That's what I'm talking about."

Lynda sighed as she knew very well what was coming next. Both Vanessa and Darcy had been after her for years to find the right man and settle down. "You mean time for marriage and babies?"

"What else?"

Lynda grimaced. "You know I don't want those things. A husband and kids would only tie me down and make me miserable. Gideon, my coworker, is a prime example of what I'm talking about. He's only twenty-seven, but he has a four-year-old son, and most of the evenings he doesn't go out anywhere because he stays home to be a father."

"Sounds like a real man to me."

A real man? Well, if he was a little older, maybe. But he was six years younger than she was and had this straitlaced attitude about life. Sure, he was cute. But even if his age was closer to hers, they were far too different to ever be more than friends.

"Gideon is a nice guy." She took a careful sip of the hot coffee. "A good guy—actually."

"Hmm. I see. That's why you have him crossed off your list," Vanessa said knowingly.

"I don't have a list." She sounded cross and that wasn't like her at all. She was accustomed to both sisters razzing her about men and her dating habits. Normally it never struck a nerve, but tonight, for some reason, she didn't want to think about men.

No doubt, Lynda. You've worn yourself out thinking about Mr. Knight.

Vanessa's reply shut out the taunting voice in Lynda's head.

"No. Your motto is just whoever strikes your fancy at the moment."

"Oh, Van, you're being ridiculous now," Lynda retorted. "But I did meet someone last night…uh, wait—let me tell you first about Mr. Creepy."

"Sounds like a real winner," Vanessa said with sarcasm.

"He was dressed like Captain Hook, and the only thing I could really see about his face was his eyes. They were the beady kind. I'm surprised the pupils weren't vertical like a snake's. But I did dance with him one time."

"Why? What was so bad about him?"

"My coworkers asked me that very question, but I don't have a reasonable answer. He just had an eerie aura about him. I wouldn't trust him as far as I could throw him. And he kept asking questions about the dinosaur dig like he was very interested in it."

"Is that so strange? He might be a paleontologist."

Lynda snorted. "I doubt Captain Hook could spell the word, much less be one. He was the sleazy sort. Like he'd try to make a dollar off of his own grandmother."

"Then why in the world did you dance with the man?"

"Oh, you know me. It's my nature to be sociable. Anyway, it was in the back of my mind I could've had him pegged all wrong and he was a big contributor to the dinosaur fund. So I did my best to be friendly."

"Oh. All for the cause. I get it."

"Well, there was no harm done. Once the dance was over he went on his way, and I wasn't bothered with him again. Shortly after Hook disappeared was when I encountered Mr. Knight." She drew in a bracing breath as the thought of their meeting still had the power to jolt her nervous system. "I'm telling you, Van, I've not been the same since. I've never been in an earthquake, but this had to be on par."

"What? Are you sober?"

The comical confusion in her sister's voice caused Lynda to chuckle. "I couldn't be more sober. The whole meeting was really indescribable. I've never been kissed like that in my entire life. And you know me, sis—I've done plenty of kissing in my day."

"Kissed? I thought you were dancing!"

"Uh, we were dancing." She sighed as her memory replayed the way she'd seemingly floated across the floor in Mr. Knight's arms. "You see, toward the end of the song, he twirled me beneath his arm and somehow my toe caught and I sort of fell into his arms."

"Oh, just sort of," Vanessa said sardonically. "A good dancer like you? Sure. Don't you mean you intentionally stumbled? What else can a girl do when she's dancing with an incredibly handsome guy?"

Smiling to herself, Lynda didn't have to close her eyes to summon up the knight's image. It was burned into her memory along with his sizzling kiss.

"To be honest, Van, I couldn't see much of his face. Only his eyes and mouth. Both of which were extremely nice."

There was a long pause, and then Vanessa asked, "Didn't you know this guy? Tenacity is a small town, and you're acquainted with just about everyone who lives around here."

"Honestly, Van, I don't have a clue to his identity. So you see why I'm going a little crazy? I've never felt anything like that kiss. It was like I was transported to some other world. Now I'm on a mission to find him."

"And if you do find him, then what? I can't imagine you going up to him and asking for a test kiss. You know, like the prince went around trying to fit the slipper on his mystery woman."

"Well, I like your idea, but I think it would have to be a spontaneous kiss, not planned. Otherwise it wouldn't be the same. And that's the whole point of finding the man. I need to determine if what I felt was real or just a…magical glow from the party."

After another short stretch of silence, Van said, "You called him Mr. Knight earlier. Does that mean he was dressed as a knight in shining armor? The roundtable kind?"

"Exactly. And the only thing I have to go on is a key chain he dropped at my feet as he was turning to leave. And now—I need to find him. Or find something to zap the whole incident out of my mind."

"Forget about finding him, sis. My advice is to go make yourself a couple of strong screwdrivers. And I'm not talking about the kind that goes in the toolbox."

Lynda groaned. "But, Van, you're the one who's always wanting me to find the right man. Maybe Mr. Knight is the right one."

"Trust your big sister on this," Van said. "One wild kiss does not make Mr. Right. You should know that by now."

No one knew it better than Lynda. She'd dated men who were experts in the art of kissing. But expertise didn't necessarily make a kiss feel magical.

"You're right," she muttered. "I need to try to be sensible about this."

"Where a man is concerned, I've not known you to

be sensible. But I'm glad to hear you're going to try. I've got to get off the phone, Lynda. My spaghetti is ready to drain, and it sounds like the kids are breaking up the furniture in the living room. Bye, sis."

Vanessa disconnected the call, and Lynda thoughtfully placed her phone on the tabletop.

The lives of Lynda's two sisters revolved around their husbands and children. Lynda couldn't imagine how it would feel to come home to the same man every night and stare across the dinner table at him while the kids smeared food everywhere and yelled at each other. Where was the excitement and romance in that?

When your sisters wake up in the morning they know their man is going to be lying next to them. When you wake up you're alone.

The mocking voice in her head had Lynda pressing her lips together until they formed a hard line. Damn it. She didn't want to wake up and see the same man's face next to hers every morning! Frankly, she didn't understand why she was having these sappy thoughts in the first place. They weren't like her. Not at all.

Ignoring the last of the coffee in her cup, she left the kitchen and walked straight to the closet in her bedroom. There was no reason she needed to stay home tonight and be tormented with images that didn't pertain to her life.

Thirty minutes later, wearing a pair of tight jeans and a white silky blouse beneath a black faux-fur jacket, she drove downtown to Central Avenue, through the center of town until she reached the Grizzly Bar. There, she turned onto a driveway that led to a parking lot behind the building.

After parking her car between two pickup trucks, she walked around to the entrance at the front of the building, which consisted of a large orange door flanked by two weather beaten benches. A rough facade of bricks made of natural stone covered the exterior walls and added to the rustic appearance of the classic old saloon.

When Lynda stepped through the door, a country music tune about a man done wrong was playing on the jukebox. Several customers, most of them older men who worked on local ranches, were seated at the long bar. Some were enjoying long neck bottles of beer, while others had squatty tumblers of whiskey. A few couples were seated in booths lining one wall. Many of the people Lynda had seen in the place before, but the only person she considered an acquaintance was sitting at the end of the bar, hunched over a mixed drink.

Making her way across the worn wooden floor, Lynda eased a hip on the vinyl-covered stool to his right. "Mind if I sit down?" she asked.

The older man in the battered gray cowboy hat glanced her way. As soon as he recognized it was Lynda, a toothy grin split his face. "Well, hello, sweetheart. What are you doing out on such a cold night?"

She let out short laugh. "It never gets too cold for me, Artie. And I was feeling a bit of cabin fever tonight, so here I am. What are you doing here at Grizzly's tonight? Why aren't you home with that pretty wife of yours?"

With a shake of his head, he said, "'Cause she's gone

to Bozeman to visit her sister. I've had to cook for myself the past two nights. Guess what I fixed for myself."

She tapped a finger against her chin and pretended to think hard. "Probably tacos or *carne guisada* and tortillas from Castillo's Restaurant."

Art chuckled. "You're a good guesser, Lynda."

She shot him a knowing smile. "I'll bet you can cook, too. You just don't want to."

"Right again," he said with a short laugh.

Behind the counter, the big bearded bartender, Dale Clutterbuck ambled slowly down to Lynda. "What you having tonight, pretty lady?"

"A screwdriver. And make it a strong one, Dale—my nerves are jangled," she told him.

Batting a hand through the air, he clicked his tongue with disapproval. "Too many divorces, Lynda. You need a more uplifting job. Like nursing."

Lynda laughed. "I always did dream about carrying bed pans and giving nasty old men like you two a bath. No, thanks. I'll stick with being a divorce lawyer."

"Well, it was just a suggestion," he said with a chuckle. "I'll go make that screwdriver for you. And heavy on the vodka."

The bartender moved away, and Lynda looked at Artie. "If you want to know the truth, I'm out tonight looking for a man."

The old cowboy grunted. "Any man, or one particular one?"

"A particular one. But I don't know who he is or exactly what he looks like."

"You sound like a mixed-up woman."

That was an understatement, Lynda thought. "I know it sounds silly, but I met this guy at the masquerade ball and his face was mostly covered. I'm trying to find out who he is. You didn't happen to go to the ball, did you?"

He snorted a laugh. "I can dance, Lynda, but only the kind of feet shuffling you'd see here in the bar. Besides, Junie was gone. She likes to go to those fancy parties. Not my cup of tea, though."

"Well, do you know if any of the men you work with on the ranch went to the ball?"

"Didn't hear any of them mention it. But that's not sayin' much. This recent bad weather has all of us going in different directions. I've been spreading hay from daylight to after dark."

She sighed. "Well, just thought I'd ask."

During a lunch break at the office, Lynda had heard Gideon mention the long hours he and his dad had been putting in on their Pine Ridge Ranch. There were times she wondered why Gideon had remained in the ranching business with his father, Ash. He made a nice living as a lawyer, dealing mostly in wills and land-property cases. There wasn't any need for him to do ranch work on the side. She imagined he did it for his parents' sake, to help them keep Pine Ridge going. Or maybe he liked being a cowboy.

Funny that Gideon should cross her mind tonight when her thoughts were already so consumed with Mr. Knight. Most often she didn't think about Gideon, unless something at work forced them to put their heads together.

Dale served her drink, and as she took a slow sip,

she swiveled the stool just enough to give her a view of the interior of the bar, which was dimly lit by a chandelier made of deer antlers. Of all the younger men in the place, she didn't see any with the build of her mystery knight. But then, he probably didn't frequent bars like Grizzly's. For some unexplainable reason, she'd gotten the impression he was high society. He probably drove over to Bronco Heights to a fancy establishment to dine and drink. Or perhaps he lived on the west side of the state in Butte or Great Falls and came here to Tenacity just to see what the upcoming dinosaur dig was all about.

You're guessing, Lynda. You want to think your knight is a prince. But mostly likely he runs heavy equipment and drinks moonshine from a mason jar. Those type of guys have magical kisses, too, you know.

The voice going off in Lynda's head caused her to pause and think. Exactly what sort of person would her knight be if she did actually find him? Would he be someone who held the same hopes and dreams as hers? Would his goals in life be similar to those she'd made for herself?

She took a long sip of the cocktail and mentally shook her head. Of course she'd want to associate herself with the man, she thought crossly. Why wouldn't she? He'd danced and kissed like a dream. He couldn't be all bad.

Forty-five minutes later, Artie had left for home and she was finishing the last of a second screwdriver when a tall, blond man with a chocolate-brown cowboy hat and ruddy cheeks eased onto the stool next to her.

"Hey, Lynda. What luck seeing you here tonight."

She glanced over to see, Mickey, one of her old high school boyfriends she still dated occasionally. Normally her pulse would pick up its pace when she ran into Mick, as she'd always called him. But tonight it wasn't so much as making a flicker in her heartbeat.

Must've been those damn screwdrivers Van had advised her to drink, she thought regretfully.

Smiling at him, she said, "Hello, Mick. When did you get back in town?"

"Only this afternoon. I'm here for about nine days. The rig I've been working on finished up, and the workover crew has taken over. Thought I'd drive over to Tenacity and see everyone."

Mickey had worked in the oil field for the past several years and had recently been promoted to a driller. He made great money, but he worked such long hours he rarely had time to spend his wages.

"Oh, I see. So I imagine you're staying with your folks while you're in town."

He nodded. "Yeah, I let my apartment go a few months back. I'm gone so much I didn't see any point of keeping the place."

"And with no gas or oil exploration happening around here you have to leave Tenacity to find work," she said ruefully. "It's the same old story all around town, Mick. The only businesses that are holding steady in this area are the farms and ranches."

"Well, that's what this part of the county is known for," he reasoned, then arched a brow at her. "But what is this I've been hearing about a dinosaur dig? My parents mentioned it to me earlier this evening. Is this for real?"

Nodding, she placed her empty glass on the bar. Dale quickly retrieved it and took Mickey's order for a beer.

Lynda said, "Your parents told you right. After those dinosaur bones were found a few months ago, people are getting a bit interested in the fact that there might be more. So we're thinking we should turn the whole idea into a profit-maker for the town. We want to bring tourists, scientists, geologists, paleontologists, and whoever else might be interested to Tenacity. An influx of people would mean an influx of money. And you know how much this community needs it."

"I noticed you said *we*. Are you in on this dinosaur project?"

"I'm helping out in ways I can," she told him.

A few minutes ago a young woman sitting in one of the booths had loaded the jukebox with more money, and now as another song began to play, Mickey raised a questioning brow at her.

"Feel like a dance?" he asked.

Why not? She'd come to Grizzly's tonight to lift her mood, she thought.

"Sure," she told him. "I'm always ready for a dance."

He reached for her hand, and as he led her to a small area of the wooden floor reserved for dancers, Lynda couldn't prevent her thoughts from going back to the masquerade ball. She'd danced with one man after another throughout the evening, but only one had stuck in her mind. Nothing like this had ever happened to her, and while the experience was somewhat fascinating she was also annoyed to have the incident preoccupying her thoughts.

Mickey was a strong guy with broad shoulders and muscled arms acquired not from hours in the gym but rather lifting iron drilling pipe along with heavy booms and chains. Lynda rested her cheek against his chest and tried to lose herself in the music and the warmth of his body.

But it wasn't working. Those euphoric moments she'd experienced with the mystery man continued to pop into her head.

She desperately needed to find Mr. Knight, she thought. She had to believe he could cure the strange longings she'd been experiencing. But was finding her princely knight only a hopeless fairytale?

She was sick. That was the problem, she decided. A medical reason was making her behave totally out of character. But what kind of doctor could fix what ailed her?

Chapter Three

"Daddy, can I stay home from school again today and ride Champ?"

Gideon looked over at his son. For the past ten minutes, he'd been ignoring the pile of scrambled eggs on his plate. Instead, he'd chomped his way through two pieces of toast covered with strawberry jam. Normally, Gideon wouldn't have allowed Scotty the second piece of toast without downing the eggs first. But since he'd been feeling a bit under the weather yesterday, Gideon let the behavior slide this one time.

"No. You missed school yesterday. You need to go today. Besides, it's too cold to ride Champ."

Scotty pursed his lips in disapproval. "I can wear my coat," he argued. "And anyway I might get a fever again. Then I'd need to stay home."

"If you developed a fever again, then you sure couldn't ride a horse out in the cold. You'd have to go to bed," Gideon told him.

"Aww shucks, then I don't want to get a fever."

"I don't want you to get one, either. Now hurry up and go brush your teeth. We need to leave in a few minutes."

Rising from his seat at the kitchen table, he carried

his dirty plate over to the sink. There wasn't time now to load the dishwasher. It was a ten-minute drive to the highway where Scotty caught the school bus. Then as soon as he waved his son off, he had to drive back and help his dad load a trailer with alfalfa bales before he could get dressed and head to the law office in town.

To say Gideon was a busy man was putting it mildly. But he liked having his days full and filled with a purpose. He sure didn't need idle time to sit around and daydream about Lynda. She was hardly the type of woman he needed in his life. Besides, he'd be the last man she'd ever take a romantic interest in.

While Gideon stacked the remaining dirty dishes in the sink and put away the breakfast fixings, he had a pang of guilt for how much he was away from Scotty. The kid deserved more love and attention. For the umpteenth time he thought how nice it would be for Scotty to have a mother on a full-time basis. Not one that he only visited every other weekend. He'd give Cecily credit though—she'd been trying hard to be a good mother to Scotty, but because her time with him was limited, she often went overboard. Instead of simply spending quality time with him, she thought she needed to take him places or buy him things.

Scotty had been less than a year old when he and Cecily had divorced, and since then Gideon had held primary custody of his son. Cecily had never really been cut out to be a mother. A trait that Gideon should have recognized long before they'd married, but he hadn't. She'd been a fragile little blonde with an innocent face and the ability to act her way through any lie she needed to concoct to defend her behavior.

At the time they'd married, Gideon had still been living in the main ranch house with his parents. His plans had been to stay there until he'd completed law school and he and Cecily had gotten their marriage firmly planted on solid ground. But then, in spite of using birth control, she'd gotten pregnant on their honeymoon, and the coming baby had changed everything.

Cecily had insisted she couldn't care for a baby with his mother constantly peering over her shoulder. She wanted a home of their own, where she could be the child's sole caretaker. Gideon had gone into debt to get this three-bedroom house built a quarter mile away from the main ranch house. Not that the effort had helped salvage a marriage that had been doomed practically from the start, he thought grimly.

But he was long over Cecily. Once he'd learned she'd been cheating on him with other men, the love he'd felt for her had died an instant death. And now? Yeah, he'd very much like to give Scotty a full time stepmother. He longed to have a woman at his side, one who would care about his job at Fiske and Jones along with his devotion to the family ranch. But even if he could find a woman who'd be satisfied to live out here in the country with him and a young boy, he still wanted his heart to go *kaboom* when he looked at her. To feel his boots lifting off the floor whenever he kissed her.

Like when he and Lynda had locked lips two nights ago. He'd never in his life experienced anything close to the electricity that had jolted all the way from his head to his feet. Now he couldn't quit thinking about her or longing to repeat the kiss. And to make matters more awkward, she was trying to learn the identity of the man in the suit of armor costume. How could he ever tell her? It would be too humiliating to confess to her now.

"Daddy, I'm ready to go!"

Scotty's yell from the living room broke into Gideon's wandering thoughts, and he quickly plucked his hat off a peg near the door and jammed it on his head. He had work to do that didn't include hopeless daydreams.

The law offices of Fiske and Jones were on the far north end of Central Avenue in a building with a narrow front with a cedar-lapped facade and a glass door with *Fiske and Jones Law* written at eye level. Beneath the overhang of the roof, three wooden rocking chairs, worn smooth from years of use and harsh weather, sat to the left side of the door, while to the right, a juniper bush grew in a wooden half barrel.

Behind the building was a graveled parking lot where the staff parked their vehicles. To the right side of the building and three steps below ground level, a single wooden door led into a small cloak room equipped with a closet and storage lockers. Beyond the cloak room, a long hallway ran through the center of the building. On either side of the narrow corridor, doors opened to small private offices.

When Gideon walked past the break room, he noticed it was empty, which meant Aaron Fiske and Basil Jones had already arrived. Not that the two older men were taskmasters. Neither man expected everyone to be at their desk at nine on the dot. But sitting around chatting over a cup of coffee wasn't exactly a good look for any of the staff.

Inside Gideon's office, he took off his hat and coat and hung them on a coat tree in the corner. His desk faced a wide window that looked over a quiet side street, along with a vacant lot where firework stands were usually set up ahead of the town's Fourth of July celebrations. Two wooden straight-backed chairs sat in front of his desk to supply seating for clients. Along the right wall, two tall metal file cabinets held copies of property cases that dated far back to the early days of Tenacity. Recently, Mary had been trying to put some of the ancient files on computer so they could do away with the paper copies. But she was so busy with other tasks, she had little time to devote to that job. Atop the file cabinets sat two potted philodendrons that had grown nearly to the floor since he'd started work here at Fiske and Jones. His mother had insisted on giving him the plants, saying they'd help keep the air in the room filtered.

For the most part, Gideon didn't have a secretary. He dealt with his own calls, messages, and typing that needed to be done. Tenacity wasn't exactly overflowing with folks who needed law services, so the firm tried to cut corners wherever possible. Actually, Lynda was the busiest of them all. Which was sad to think there were that many divorcing couples in town.

Ten minutes after he'd sat down at his desk and fired up his computer, a light knock sounded on his door. When he looked up, he was a bit surprised to see her walking into the room. She rarely sought him for any reason, but then, she was the veteran lawyer, not him. And she sure didn't look to him for purely social reasons.

"Hi, Gideon. Am I interrupting?"

Lynda would never know it, but she'd been interrupting his thoughts for more than two years now. And this morning she looked particularly lovely in a soft lavender sweater and a black skirt that covered the tops of her black leather boots. Usually, her long auburn hair fell loose against her back, but today part of the top was pulled up and clipped with a shiny silver clamp.

"Not at all," he told her. "I'm just now getting my morning started."

She glanced at his desktop. "I don't see a coffee mug. Didn't you want some? Mary brought in some freshly ground beans. It's super good."

"I might get a cup later. I was running a little late this morning. Dad needed help loading hay."

She stepped closer to the front of his desk, and her perfume drifted over to him. She smelled like a lovely spring morning, all sunshine and flowers.

"Oh. So how is your little boy? Was he able to go to school this morning?"

Up until yesterday, he couldn't recall Lynda ever mentioning Scotty. Frankly, he'd not been sure she'd even known he had a son, so it surprised him to hear her inquire about him again today.

"He's fine. Thanks for asking. Actually, he wanted to stay home and ride his horse instead of go to school. He's a typical boy."

A wry smile touched her lips. "I know what you mean. When I babysit for my sister's three boys, I usually end up being a referee." She shook in an exaggerated motion. "Kids are a jolt to my nervous system."

He'd heard her say something to that effect before, and he wondered if not wanting kids around was part of the reason she'd never married or been engaged. Once some men reached a certain age, they realized they wanted children, and if Lynda shied away from having kids, he could see where there would be an incompatible issue.

"Scotty can be a pill at times. But he brings me a lot of joy." Glancing away from her, he asked as casually as possible. "Have you had any luck finding the identity of your knight from the masquerade ball?"

Releasing a sigh, she eased into one of the chairs in front of his desk. "No! And it's driving me crazy. I've asked all the women who were working the refreshment table and the souvenir table, but none of them had any idea who he was. Two of the ladies remembered seeing him toward the end of the ball, and one of them, Susie Wainscott, thought he might be Richard Grover."

"Richard Grover! No way!" he burst out before he could catch himself.

Her brows peaked as she looked at him. "You weren't at the ball. There's no way you would know if the knight was Richard."

He cleared his throat and focused his gaze on the scene beyond the window. "Well, I— Just think about it, Lynda. Richard is a farmer and a shy one, at that. He rarely shows his face in town."

"But he's divorced. He could be looking for a woman. But you're right. I told Susie there was no chance it was Richard. So I've struck out so far."

"If you want my advice—"

"As a lawyer or a man?" she interrupted with the question.

Did she ever really see him as a man? Sometimes he wondered. "Both," he answered.

She crossed her legs and smiled at him. "Okay. Let me hear this advice."

Shrugging, he said, "You need to forget about the mystery knight. He's just a party phantom, not a man you need to hang your hopes on."

Especially when he knew for certain that she'd never go for a man like himself. She wanted a guy who'd take her out dancing and be a partner at charity functions, not a boring family man.

"Hmm. I'm interested to hear how you'd know this," she said. "Especially since you don't know Mr. Knight's identity."

He needed to keep his mouth shut. Otherwise she was going to become mighty suspicious.

Plucking a pen from a can on his desk, he absently rolled it between his palms. "You're right. I don't know him. I'm only thinking he most likely lives far away from Tenacity and just came for the party—to contribute."

"You could very well be right. But if he came for the party, then he might be a frequent visitor to Tenacity," she reasoned. "And if he was interested enough to contribute to the Dinosaur Center, then it stands to reason he might show up when the dig actually takes place."

Oh, he'd show up all right, Gideon thought. Scotty was already excited about the idea of digging for dinosaur bones. Gideon hadn't yet explained to his son that the actual digging would be limited to professionals.

"Could be," he admitted. "But how would you recognize him?"

She laughed under her breath, and the sexy sound shivered down his backbone.

"You've got me there. I suppose I'd have to go around asking every man who resembles Mr. Knight's build for a kiss."

The notion caused him to choke, and he coughed a couple of times before he could attempt to speak.

"Are you okay, Gideon?"

He swallowed hard and dismissed her concern with a wave of his hand. "I'm fine. I just got a little dry. I guess I should have poured myself a cup of Mary's coffee."

"Well, the reason I came in to see you this morning is to let you know that Basil has asked a favor of you and me. And frankly, I'm glad he did. I've been trying to help with this dinosaur promotion ever since the idea came up, and this is giving me more of an opportunity to throw my time and effort into it."

He studied her thoughtfully. "I wasn't aware Basil was directly involved with the dinosaur project."

"You're forgetting he's one of Tenacity's city councilmen. And he's all for the campaign of illuminating Tenacity and seeing the town prosper."

Gideon said, "I see. So where do you and I come in?"

She smiled at him, and Gideon could hardly keep his eyes off her lips and the tiny little dimples bracketing both corners.

"I've been doing some pro bono legal work for the Dinosaur Center, but that's not exactly what Basil is asking for now. It seems the masquerade ball has received a lot of media attention and donations have been pouring in. The volunteer committee for the Dinosaur Center needs more help dealing with how to make the most of the contributions. You know, figuring out where every available penny should go—that sort of thing. Basil would like for us to figure out a marketing idea to promote the dig with using as little funds as possible."

"In other words, he wants us to work a miracle," Gideon replied.

She shook a shaming finger at him. "If it takes a miracle, then you and I will just have to create one."

A miracle? That was exactly what he was going to need to keep his head on straight around this woman, he thought.

He leveled a pointed look at her. "And when would the two of us be doing this volunteering miracle work? It's not like I can stay after office hours, Lynda. I have Scotty to care for and responsibilities on the ranch."

"Basil understands your situation, Gideon. So he's offering to let us off two hours early each day to contribute our effort to the cause."

"Are you kidding?" he asked, then frowned as another thought struck him. "And what about Aaron? He's just as much our boss as Basil. He might not want us giving out free solicitor work."

"Wrong. Aaron is all in on the idea."

"Then I suppose our salaries will be docked for the time we're away from the office."

Her smile turned impish. "Gideon, you're such a fuddy-duddy. Aaron and Basil aren't going to cut our salaries. If anything, they'll probably give us a bonus when this is all over. Just consider the whole picture. Tenacity's economy is going to benefit everyone, including this law firm. And our bosses love this hometown of theirs as much as I do."

That was one thing he could say about Lynda—she loved Tenacity and was proud of the community, even though it had fallen on hard times in recent years. And he admired, among many other things, her loyalty and genuine concern for the townspeople.

A half grin twisted his lips. "Then I guess you'd better count me in on this deal."

"Great! I know we'll make a good team. Maybe we might even be able to come up with some new ideas for fundraisers."

"Uh, Lynda, sorry to be a fuddy-duddy again, but don't you think the citizens of Tenacity have given about all they can give to the cause? We don't want to overtax their wallets."

"Of course we don't. That's why you and I need to put our heads together and think up something that would draw in outside money." She batted a dismissive hand through the air. "But we'll work on that idea later. So can you start tomorrow afternoon? I told Basil you'd probably need to get things situated at home before you begin."

Gideon's head was spinning. Not just from the idea he was going to be devoting hours of volunteer work but that he'd be doing it with Lynda. *The* Lynda who made his heart do silly somersaults.

"Thanks for the consideration. I suppose I can start tomorrow. But I would like to know about one thing," he told her.

"Oh? What's that?"

"Why didn't Basil come to me about this instead of sending you?"

Rising from the chair, she rested her palms on the edge of the desk, and with a wicked little smile leaned slightly toward him. "He thought I might be more persuasive."

Basil Jones was hardly a fool. He, and most everyone else who was acquainted with Lynda, knew she could charm the wings off a honeybee.

The smile he gave her probably looked helpless, but he hoped she wouldn't notice. "I'm an easy target."

"I wouldn't say that." She straightened away from his desk and started toward the door. "Thanks, Gideon. You're a stand-up guy."

"Yeah, well, I try to be."

She went out the door, and as she shut it behind her, Gideon leaned back in his chair and scrubbed his face with both hands. Was he dreaming, or what? Him and Lynda working together? How in the world was he going to hide his crush on her? Especially if she continued to bring up her mystery knight and that humdinger of a kiss. He hated deceiving her and didn't know how much longer he could continue to hide the fact that *he* was her knight.

Blowing out a heavy breath, he pulled up a will he'd been working on and tried to focus on the legal terms he'd written so far. But it was hard to see the words when Lynda's smiling lips kept parading across the monitor screen in his mind.

"Knock, knock!"

Her voice interrupted his daydreaming, and he looked around to see her entering the room again. This time she was carrying a tall red mug with steam curling up from the top.

"What is this?"

"A cup of Mary's coffee. Since you hadn't drunk any yet, I thought I'd bring you a cup as a thank-you for agreeing to volunteer with me."

Since the downturn of Tenacity's economy, the townspeople had rallied to help, and for the past few years, all sorts of crusaders had been held to prop up businesses that were on the verge of failing. Most recently the library. Lynda had been involved with many of those efforts, but she seemed to be particularly excited about the Dinosaur Center.

She placed the cup on his desk, and he reached for it. "Thanks, Lynda. This is nice. And you put cream in it. How did you guess?"

Chuckling, she turned to go. "I don't guess. I take notes. It's the lawyer in me."

Just before she reached the door to leave, he said, "This Dinosaur Center thing must mean a lot to you."

She looked over her shoulder at him. "It means very much to me." Her expression suddenly thoughtful, and she turned so that she was facing him. "You might have heard me mention this before, and maybe you haven't. My dad owned and operated a housing-construction business, and my mom taught elementary school here in Tenacity. But five years ago—before you came to work here at the firm—my parents had to sell the home they'd lived in for over thirty years and move away just to survive. I don't want that to happen to any more of our longtime citizens. It's heartbreaking."

The Lynda Slater he'd known so far was always laughing and smiling and seemingly enjoying life to the fullest. He'd never seen her in such a serious mood—unless it was in the courtroom, and then she was like a tigress fighting for her cubs. This caring, sensitive side of Lynda was the part of her that attracted Gideon far more than just her beautiful face and sexy figure. And he hoped that other people could see her compassion for helping those that needed it the most.

"You're right," he said. "Helping the town and its citizens is a good reason to throw our efforts into the cause."

The smile returned to her face, and Gideon realized he'd do most anything to please her. A fact that probably made him the biggest chump in Tenacity.

"Now you're talking, Gideon."

She gave him a wink, then went on out the door. After it closed behind her, Gideon sat back in his desk chair and let out a pent up breath.

A cup of coffee, a wink, and a smile and he was already a goner.

Face it, Gideon—you've been gone on Lynda from the first day you laid eyes on her.

Yeah, that much was true, he thought ruefully. But maybe spending this exclusive time with her in these coming days would be a good way to get her out of his system.

Or make him want her even more.

Later that evening when Lynda left the office building and slipped into the driver's seat of her car, she was humming a happy little tune about a woman finding love for a second time. She didn't know why her mood was light or what had even caused the song to enter her head. She certainly wasn't looking for love even for a first time, much less a second. Her life was good. She didn't need a bunch of emotional drama to mess it all up.

And after today, Lynda was convinced there was not one chance in hell she'd ever sign her name on a marriage license. Over the course of her career as a divorce lawyer, she'd seen plenty of nasty splits and despicable behavior from both partners, but today when her high school English teacher, Mamie Rodgers, had walked into her office and announced she wanted Lynda to handle her divorce, she'd been shocked, angry, disillusioned, and all of the above. Mamie and her husband, Wallace, had been married for more than fifty years. Lynda would have nominated them to be the poster couple of a perfect marriage. Instead, she heard that Mamie just learned Wallace had been keeping a mistress for years in a small town located somewhere between Tenacity and Bronco.

The facts of the Rodgers divorce case only emphasized Lynda's determination to remain single and uncommitted. Mamie had borne the man three children and had worked tirelessly as a teacher to help the family be financially secure. And at seventy years old, Mamie was still a beautiful and intelligent woman. There wasn't a mean bone in her body, and Lynda would feel safe in betting the woman had always complied with anything and everything her husband wanted.

That was the kind of reward a woman got for loving a man, she thought dryly. A kick in the teeth. No. She didn't want that for herself. Even a few kisses from her dreamy knight wouldn't be enough to lead Lynda to the matrimony altar.

She pushed a button on the steering wheel to bring up the volume on the radio before she flipped on the blinker and made a left off Central Avenue. Before she'd left her office, she'd made a call to her best friend, Ruby McKinley, to see if she was going to be home or would mind if Lynda stopped by for a few minutes for a chat and to see her and the kids.

Normally, Lynda wouldn't bother to call, she'd simply drive by and make herself at home. But since Ruby had married Julian Sanchez, the woman's life had changed. And in spite of Lynda's aversion to the idea of marriage, she had to admit that in Ruby's case, her life had changed for the better. Now that she was wearing Julian's ring, she was glowing with happiness.

At Ruby's house, Lynda made her way to the front porch, but before she had time to press the doorbell, the door flew open and the pretty blonde enfolded her in an affectionate hug. "Okay, stranger, come in and tell me everything!"

She grabbed Lynda's hand and tugged her into the house and straight to the living room. Emery, her five-year-old daughter was sitting on the floor playing with a group of plastic farm animals and a little red barn with a white railed fence erected around it. As soon as the girl spotted Lynda, she jumped to her feet and ran straight to her.

"Auntie Lynda!"

Laughing, Lynda scooped the child up into her arms and smacked a kiss on her rosy cheek. "How's my girl? I think you've grown since last week!" she exclaimed.

"Mommy says I'm gonna need new shoes 'cause my feet are getting big!"

"Oh my! That means you are growing! Before your mommy knows it you'll be asking for a pair of stiletto heels."

Ruby let out a good-natured groan. "Lynda! Don't give her ideas. She'll be dating age long before I want her to be."

Emery wrinkled her nose as her little fingers played with Lynda's auburn hair lying against her shoulder. "What are those shoes, Auntie Lynda? Are they pretty? With bows?"

Laughing, Lynda danced her around the room. "Of course they're pretty. And some of them have bows. But you can only wear them when you grow to be as big as your mommy."

The girl shot Lynda a perplexed look. "Does Mommy wear them?"

With another chuckle, Lynda glanced over at her friend. Ruby was a natural beauty, with blond hair and blue eyes. She was the pretty and wholesome girl next door, not the *stiletto, glamour girl* type.

"I'm not sure. She might have a pair hiding out in the closet somewhere." She placed the child back on the floor, then glanced around. "Where's your brother, Jay?"

"In his pen. Asleep." Emery pointed to an area beyond a love seat.

"Sorry, Ruby. Why didn't you shush me? I'll have a look to see if I woke him up with my laughing."

"Don't worry. If he was awake, he'd be letting us know about it by now."

Ruby tiptoed over to a small area penned off with expandable fencing and peered at the little boy. Lying on his back, on a bed made of pillows and quilts, he was covered with a thick blue blanket. One fist was resting against his chin.

Lynda gazed down at the slumbering child for a moment, then walked back over to where Ruby had taken a seat on the couch.

"He's sleeping peacefully," Lynda told her.

Ruby patted the cushion next to her. "Sit down. Or would you like to go to the kitchen for coffee or cake or something? I have a roast cooking in the oven. You're welcome to stay and eat."

"No, thanks. I'll make myself a light supper when I get home. Something without sugar. Mary brought homemade cookies to the office today, and I made a hog of myself."

"So have you been busy? Why haven't I heard from you?"

"Sorry. I've been extra busy. And today—Ruby, there are times I hate my job."

"Then why do you do it?"

She heaved out a heavy breath. "To help people get through a bad time in their lives. I mean, by the time they come to me, they've already decided they want a divorce. So they need advice and legal assistance in order to make the split of assets fair, and in the case of the children—well, you know all about these things. You've gone through your own divorce. But today, Ruby, you're not going to believe who walked into my office."

"Who?"

"Mamie Rodgers."

Ruby's brows shot up. "You mean Mrs. Rodgers, the high school English teacher?"

Lynda nodded. "The one and only. She taught me in high school, and I've always loved her dearly."

"She wants a divorce?" Ruby asked incredulously. "But I see her and her husband together all over town. They seem happy together!"

"They were happy until Mamie found out about Wallace's mistress."

"At his age? Is this one of your jokes?" she exclaimed, then groaned. "Why am I questioning you? I guess age doesn't matter to a cheater."

Shaking her head, Lynda reached over and patted Ruby's arm. She knew her friend had to be thinking of her own ex-husband, who'd been a pro at hiding his dalliances with other women. "No need for you to think about that now. You have Julian, and he's a great husband to you. And a wonderful father to the children."

Smiling, Ruby held up her left hand and wiggled her fingers, causing the light to glitter off her wedding ring. "I happen to think so," she said dreamily, then cast a puzzled look at Lynda. "But I can't understand your way of thinking. If you believe Julian will be a good husband I can trust, then why do you insist most all other men are stinkers? Only to be enjoyed and not taken seriously?"

Lynda shrugged. "Because the majority of them are stinkers—that's why. And it's much safer and more sensible to just enjoy a good-looking man. There's no reason to throw your heart away on a lost cause."

Ruby's lips compressed to a disapproving line. "I can't be like you, Lynda. I want my heart to be involved. Otherwise the whole relationship is meaningless."

Biting back a sigh, Lynda asked wearily, "How many times have we had this same old argument?"

An affectionate smile curved Ruby's lips. "We're not arguing. We're best friends. We just have differences of opinions about men and the parts they play in our lives."

"*Play.*" Lynda latched on to that one word of Ruby's remark. "That's the key term, my friend. Men make a career out of playing. A woman should have a right to do the same."

"You do have the right. But will your commitment to your job and the center be enough for the rest of your life? Is that all you want?"

Ruby's question had Lynda glancing over to Emery. The little girl was sitting cross-legged on the area rug, playing with her farm and ranch toys. And as she watched the child carefully place a cow and lamb inside the red barn, Lynda had to admit there were times she felt maternal urges. And those times when she held Jay in her arms, felt his soft warmth and saw him smiling up at her, she wondered how it might feel to be a mother. But she didn't allow herself to hold on to the thought for more than a few seconds. She had too much going in her life to be tied down with babies.

"Maybe it is. I don't know, Ruby. Right now I'm not looking for serious love. I'm not sure I ever will be. But I am looking for a certain guy."

Ruby's expression turned hopeful. "You are? This is wonderful news. Because I'm positive once you find the right guy, everything is going to change around in that head of yours."

A light laugh slipped past Lynda's throat. "When I said I'm looking for a certain guy, I meant literally," she said, then with a thoughtful frown, asked, "Did you go to the masquerade ball? I didn't see you or Julian there, but since everyone was in disguise I could've missed you two."

Shaking her head, Ruby said, "Sorry. I forgot all about getting a costume. And as it turned out Julian had to deal with some things on the ranch that night. Plus Jay had the sniffles and I was worried he was coming down with a really bad cold. But thankfully he didn't."

"Oh. Well, it's a shame you missed it. The center was packed with people and the music was excellent. The reason I asked if you were there I thought there might have been a chance you saw my guy."

"Your guy?"

"Uh, my dance partner. I'm trying to learn his identity. I've been asking around, trying to find out who he is, but I'm not having any luck. And it's driving me insane."

"What's the deal about this one certain man? Did he donate a bunch of money or something?"

"It's possible he donated. See, anyone could donate anonymously, so his name might not have been listed on the registrar. But that's not why I need to find him. It's all about a kiss."

Ruby let out a loud groan. "I should've known."

Lynda gave her friend an impatient frown. "It wasn't just physical. It was more like…magic."

She quickly relayed to Ruby what had happened during her dance with Mr. Knight and how the kiss had affected her in a way she couldn't explain.

"So you see, I need to find this guy," Lynda continued. "I need to discover for myself if the kiss was just a one fluke wonder or if fate meant for us to be together. All day long, my clients tell me about the terrible things their husbands have done to bring them into my office. But this guy…he was my white knight. And I need to know that wasn't just a fairy tale, that there really is a good man out there."

Ruby was thoughtful for a long moment before she absently tapped a forefinger against her chin. "You know, I think you might finally be heading in the right direction."

Lynda never expected to hear this from her friend, and she looked at her skeptically. "Really? You're not being sarcastic about this?"

Smiling, Ruby reached over and gave Lynda's hand a quick squeeze. "No. I really mean this. I'm reading between the lines here, but I believe you're actually thinking about this guy in a romantic way. Am I right?"

Lynda stared at her and tried to ignore the shock stinging her thoughts. She hadn't thought beyond finding her mystery man. *Was* she thinking of him in a romantic way? No! She never allowed herself to think in those terms. Romance was too closely linked to love.

"I—uh—no! I mean, I'll admit he made a dashing, romantic figure. I just want to find him."

"And you didn't get his name? Where he was from? Anything?"

Shaking her head, she said, "While we were dancing we, uh, didn't talk. I can't speak for him, but I felt like a spell had come over me. And then, after the kiss, I didn't have a chance. All I have now is that darned key chain!" She turned a hopeful look on Ruby. "You see all kinds of people coming and going in the inn." Ruby worked the reception desk at Tenacity Inn. "Could be the man reserved a room there during the ball."

Ruby rolled her eyes. "And signed the registrar card as *Mr. Knight in Shining Armor*? There's no way of knowing if he was there."

"Unfortunately, you're right. Then can you think of someone who might know the knight's identity?"

Ruby's brows arched upward. "My first suggestion would be the people who were working at the ball or just attending. You'll just have to keep asking around."

"And making myself look like a fool," she muttered helplessly. "You probably won't believe this, but I almost considered putting an ad in the paper asking the man to reveal himself. Until I came to my senses and realized how ridiculous that would look and stopped myself."

"Thank goodness you did. I can't imagine Aaron and Basil approving of one of their lawyers going off on a wild goose chase."

Lynda shot her a look. "Is that what you think I'm doing?"

"Sorry. You do want me to be honest, don't you?"

Groaning, Lynda said, "Now you sound like Gideon. He believes everyone should be brutally honest. I think that notion stems from all the lies his ex-wife told him. At least that's what Mary has implied. Gideon doesn't talk about his private life to me. He's strictly business and walks the straight and narrow."

Ruby slanted her a knowing look. "Honesty is much better than living with lies."

Lynda could hardly argue with her friend. Ruby's life had been shattered by her ex-husband's habitual lying. "You're right, Ruby. Honest and upstanding. There's nothing wrong with a man having those things—if you can find one," she added ruefully. Of course, Gideon was honest and upstanding, she thought. But his age and staunch family lifestyle made him an incompatible choice for her.

Ruby left the couch long enough to walk over and peek at her son. Once she was satisfied he was sleeping peacefully, she returned to her seat next to Lynda.

"So other than Mamie coming in for a divorce, how have things been going at Fiske and Jones?" she asked.

"No scandalous cases to liven things up. Actually, it's been fairly humdrum. But my daily schedule is about to change. As a favor to Basil and to help Tenacity, of course, Gideon and I are going to be working together—volunteering at the Dinosaur Center."

"Now, that's interesting."

"I don't know about interesting, but it will be different. Actually, the few times Gideon and I have had to put our heads together on a case, we've managed quite well."

"Hmm. I see him around town occasionally," Ruby remarked. "He's a cute guy. Young, but you'd have to say he's already lived a lot. Marriage, divorce, raising a kid basically on his own. I can relate to what he's gone through."

"Well, I'm very thankful I can't relate. But that has nothing to do with Gideon and me working together. It's all about the Dinosaur Center. We'll make a good team."

Ruby slanted her a sly glance. "Maybe working closely with Gideon will make you forget all about the knight."

Laughing now, Lynda rose to her feet. "Gideon is like a younger brother to me. And anyway, he's exactly my opposite. As far as I know, he gets his excitement from feeding cows. He's a—well, a bit of a stuffed shirt."

"Why let that stop you?" Ruby asked. "I'm sure you've heard of the old saying—opposites attract."

Lynda laughed again. "Not in this case. But nice try, Ruby. Now, I need to head home and make myself do laundry."

Ruby stood, and after Lynda had given Emery a goodbye kiss and took one last peek at sleeping Jay, the two friends walked to the front door.

"I only want you to be happy, Lynda. You know that, don't you?"

"Of course I do. But you need to realize that what makes you happy and me happy are two totally different things."

Smiling, she planted a light kiss on Ruby's cheek. "See you later. And if you do happen to run across a knight around town somewhere, let me know."

Ruby chuckled. "You'll be the first on my to-call list."

Chapter Four

The Tenacity Dinosaur Center and Park was a short distance from town, nestled in a clearing in the woods. With some lucky weather, they'd been able to continue building the center through the winter. And now they were finally able to move out of the trailers they'd been working in and into the huge three-story cement structure with equally large windows at the entrance. Beyond it, a view of a snowcapped mountain ridge to the north rose up to meet the wide Montana sky. At the front of the building a large parking area ran adjacent to a spacious lawn separated in the middle by a concrete walkway. The lengthy sidewalk led to the entrance of the building. During the warm months, flowers and shrubs would be blooming along each side of the entrance.

And eventually they were hoping to raise enough money to source a life-sized replica of a tyrannosaurus rex to pose on the right-hand section of the lawn.

Now, as Lynda stood outside her car and waited for Gideon to depart his truck and join her on the sidewalk, she gazed up at the enormous skeleton and wondered if more actual bones could be found where the initial bones had been discovered.

"Can you imagine how frightening it would be to live in the dinosaur era? I don't think you'd feel safe taking your dog for a walk."

Gideon's voice had her glancing over her shoulder to find he'd walked directly behind her without her knowing he'd gotten so close. And seeing him outside of the office in the bright sunshine made him look entirely different than the lawyer sitting behind his desk. Or perhaps standing this close to him was giving her a chance to view him from all angles. And what Lynda was seeing was surprisingly nice. A silver-gray Stetson was pulled low on his forehead and a battered leather jacket covered his broad shoulders. Faded jeans encased his long, strong legs and ended at a pair of chocolate-brown cowboy boots.

Yep, he was all man, she decided, with his wide chest and lean waist. He was also the perfect image of a rugged cowboy. So why hadn't she noticed all of this before?

Because Gideon is six years younger than you. He has a four-year-old son. Plus, he'd be indignant if you asked him to bend the rules.

What rules? she silently shouted at the voice in her head. The only rules she went by were to keep things light and loose.

"I don't have a dog. But if I did I wouldn't be guilty of walking anywhere with creatures like T. rex hanging around," she assured him.

"Hmm. Then why have you been carrying a T. rex around with you?"

Her expression blank, she turned to face him. "What are you talking about?"

Beneath the brim of his cowboy hat, she could see a faint ruddy color staining his jaws.

"The key chain," he explained. "From the masquerade ball."

"Oh. How did you know about the key chain?" she asked, then remembered before he could reply. "Never mind that question—I remember now. You were in the break room when I was showing the trinket to everyone."

"Right. You said you'd never forget the knight in shining armor. But I've not heard you make an announcement that you've found him."

She sighed. "Unfortunately, no. Do you happen to know who the man is and you just don't want to tell me?"

He frowned. "Me? Why, no. And why would I keep something like that from you if I did?"

She tilted her head to one side as she continued to study his face. Could be that she was imagining things, but his expression looked sheepish to her.

"I'm not sure," she answered. "Except—well, if you knew the guy was a sorry character, you might lie a little to keep me from being embarrassed."

"I'm not going to lie. Besides, he could turn out to be a friend." Turning his gaze toward the building, he placed a hand at the small of her back and urged her forward. "Come on. It's cold out here, and we need to get to work."

As they walked toward the double glass doors, Lynda

couldn't ignore the warm weight of Gideon's hand resting lightly against her back. Nor could she dismiss the occasional light brush of his leg against hers. Even though he was wearing thick denim jeans and the hem of her green suede skirt fell all the way to the ankles of her boots, she was experiencing tiny shocks from the contact.

Which was crazy! This was Gideon. Her coworker. He wasn't out for fun and games. Nor was she. Not with a frosty dude like him.

Gideon hadn't been in the Dinosaur Center before, so he wasn't sure what to expect when they first entered the building. Although the museum and park were still being developed, Scotty loved reading and hearing about dinosaurs and had been persistently hounding him about when he could make a visit to the center.

"I haven't told Scotty yet about me working here in the afternoons," he told Lynda as they moved through the lobby and toward a set of stairs. "If he knew, he'd be throwing a fit to come out here with me."

She shrugged. "You could bring him out here with you one afternoon," she suggested. "It's not like we're seeing clients. We're basically our own bosses out here. I don't see a problem with it."

He'd not expected her to suggest such a thing. Especially when she was such a non-kid person. But maybe she didn't have a problem dealing with other people's kids, he thought. She just didn't want any of her own.

"I might do that. For one afternoon. He's crazy about dinosaurs and wants to learn everything about them.

And he's constantly asking me about the dig and when it might happen."

They reached the staircase, and she gestured for them to begin climbing. "The office we'll be working in is on the top floor, so we'll get a workout climbing the stairs."

"Isn't there an elevator in this place?"

"There is. But they've been working on it. Something about the electrical system."

He chuckled. "I need the exercise. Sitting at a desk all day isn't exactly my idea of work."

She cast a comical look at him. "How can a lawyer work if he isn't sitting at his desk? Unless you're walking around the courtroom, and you don't do that too often. Somehow you always manage to get your clients to settle disputes out of court. How do you do it?"

"When you put everything to them in dollars and cents, they listen and take heed. Court costs piled on a lawyer's fee isn't pleasant to deal with. And then there's always a chance they might lose the case."

"Not with you representing them."

Her comment caused him to pause on the step, and when she stopped alongside him, he looked over at her. "Are you being sarcastic?" he asked.

"Why, no." Her lips took a downward turn. "I'm serious. You're a very good lawyer."

Lynda had always been nice and pleasant to him, but he couldn't remember a time she'd actually complimented him and he was taken aback by her offhand comment.

"Thanks. So are you."

Shrugging, she said, "I suppose I am fairly good at

winning my cases. However, there are times I wonder if I'm really winning. You know what I mean?"

More often than not, Lynda's cases dealt with emotional family issues and there were times he could see how deeply she was affected by her client's misery. And no matter how hard she fought in the courtroom, he knew it bothered her to see a couple split. Especially those with children.

"Yes. Exactly. And living in Tenacity makes it especially hard because we know just about everyone who walks into the office."

"A lot of them we grew up with," she said. "Which makes it hard not to be biased."

She started up the stairs, and he kept in step with her until they reached the landing.

"We go to the right here. The office is a couple doors down," she told him.

They walked onward, and as they passed the first door Gideon noticed it was partially ajar. He could see a middle-aged woman he didn't recognize working at a computer. When they reached the second door, Lynda opened it and reached to one side to flip on a light switch.

When two strips of fluorescent lights flickered to life, she gestured toward the interior. "Ta-da! Welcome to our workspace. It's nothing fancy, but it's comfortable and serves the purpose."

He followed her into the office, where two separate desks were positioned side by side in the middle of the room. Both were equipped with computers and executive chairs, and both faced a wide plate-glass window that looked out at an endless stretch of deep woods. On one wall there were rows of built in bookshelves but no books were to be seen. However there were boxes of printer paper and other types of office supplies stacked on the bottom shelf.

"What's the printer paper used for? I don't see a printer."

"For right now there's one in Krystal's office. She's secretary to Earl Laughton, the marketing director. Most of his work is pro bono, and since he lives over in Bronco he only comes in on certain days. Hence them also needing us."

"So in other words we're keeping the marketing work going," he said with a knowing grin.

"Exactly," she said with a playful wink at him. "But mostly Krystal. Women are usually the wheels that keep things moving."

"I'll agree with that. Without Mom, my dad would have probably thrown in the towel years ago." He moved over to one of the desks. "How long have you been coming out here as a volunteer?" Gideon asked her.

She pulled off her coat and hung it on a coat tree standing in a far back corner of the room. As she rejoined him at the pair of desks, Gideon tried not to stare at the shapely figure she made in a bottle green sweater belted at the waist. He'd been around sexy looking women before. Especially when he'd been in law school. But none of them had possessed the oomph factor like Lynda. The combination of her energy and sensuality made for quite a woman.

She said, "Shortly after the first bones were discovered. At first there wasn't a whole lot to do. But now with more money coming in someone has to help make sure the funds are directed to the places most needed. And sometimes there's a bit of legal work involved, like going over contracts with construction companies, property lines, and things of that sort. Nothing is very complicated, though," she explained.

He walked to the back of the room and hung his coat and hat next to hers. When he returned to the set of desks, he asked, "Which computer do I work on? Or does it matter?"

"I've used both, so it doesn't matter at all to me. We can access the files or whatever we need from either computer, so pick the desk you want," she told him.

"Okay. I'll take this one."

He pulled out the executive chair to the right and eased his tall frame into the seat; she sank into the chair next to him. And all Gideon could think about was the minute space between them. They were close enough for him to pick up her flowery perfume, see the darker flecks of blue surrounding her pupils and the gleam on her bottom lip. How was he supposed to work under these conditions? Shut his eyes and pretend he was herding cattle through a field of wildflowers?

No, he should be concentrating on her willingness to donate her time and effort to help the dinosaur center achieve its goals, he told himself. He should be thinking of her dedication to help Tenacity and its citizens thrive again. Sure, she was a gorgeous woman. But in the end, her caring and generous nature were the things about Lynda that tugged on his emotions.

* * *

Close to an hour later, Lynda was trying to focus on an estimated cost of equipment involving the dig the center was planning when Gideon left his chair and walked over to the window.

Throughout the past hour, he'd not spoken much. Further proof they were exact opposites, she thought. Talking was one of her many joys in life, and normally Gideon's quietness would have grated on her nerves. But for some reason she wasn't bothered by his pensiveness today. Maybe that was because she'd been too busy snatching secret little glances at him from the corner of her eye.

She didn't know where her thoughts were coming from or why she was suddenly seeing Gideon in a different light, but she was totally taken aback by this new awareness of the man. Had he always looked so sexy in his jeans and boots? And she'd never noticed how his dark hair waved against the back of his neck in such an appealing way or how his brown eyes held such a sexy glint whenever he looked at her. Had Gideon changed, or had she?

The answer had to be the effects of some sort of cosmic rays from the lunar eclipse. They'd affected her vision and her ability to think clearly. At least where men were concerned.

"Gideon, did you watch the lunar eclipse the other night?"

Turning away from the window, he looked at her with faint surprise. "I did. I took Scotty out in the back yard so we could get a wide open view of the moon. It was beautiful, and my son was impressed. So far he seems to be somewhat science minded. Whether that interest will stick with him as he grows older is something only time will tell. Why do you ask if I saw the eclipse? You a science buff too?"

She laughed lightly. "No. Law has always been my thing. But I was just wondering about cosmic rays and if they can affect us here on Earth."

He returned to his desk, but he didn't take a seat in his chair. Instead he propped a hip over one corner of the desk, which instantly caused Lynda's gaze to go straight to the denim stretched across the thick muscle of his thigh.

"I don't know much about science, either. But I do know that the earth has a magnetic field that shields us from the radiation in cosmic rays."

"Oh, that's too bad." As soon as she saw his brows shoot up, she realized she sounded idiotic.

"It is? You'd rather civilization die from radiation?"

"Of course not. I just meant—I was only trying to come up with a reason for people to suddenly behave out of character."

"You have someone in mind?"

What would he think if she told him she was the one behaving out of character? That she was suddenly too strange to be working as a lawyer for Fiske and Jones?

With a silent groan, she said, "No. I, uh, have clients who behave weirdly at times. But people who are getting a divorce are usually in a weird state of mind anyway."

His lips took on a wry slant. "I can assure you divorces aren't a result of lunar eclipses."

Lynda had never really thought much about Gideon's personal life. But now, with the two of them here and basically alone, she was noticing everything about him. And she could see from the expression on his face that his own divorce had torn him.

Leaning back in her chair, she continued to study his rugged features. "Were you in love with your wife when you two divorced?"

He cocked one dark brow at her. "Why do you ask?"

She made a palms-up gesture. "Because divorce is my job. I see it every day, and there are times I suspect one or both spouses are still in love but just don't have a strong enough constitution to stay hooked."

He grimaced. "Well, in my case, I wasn't still in love with Cecily. Looking back on things now, I'm not certain I was ever truly in love with her. I guess that's an awful thing to admit. I married her and we had a child together. But I think I was more infatuated with her and the idea of being married and having a family of my own than anything." He paused and shook his head as though he wished he could shake away the memories and the mistakes. "Her cheating and lying was too much for me to take. No man wants to share his wife with other men."

Yes, Lynda could see he was a proud man, and she admired him for having the courage and strength to move on from his mistakes.

"I'm sorry. I wasn't sure that's what happened with you two," she admitted. "I'd heard Cecily was...well, a flirt, but you can hear all sorts of things around Tenacity. Most of the town's gossip I take with a grain of salt."

Sighing, he moved off the desk and began to walk aimlessly around the room. "She was too young to be a wife and mother. We'd been married only a few short months when she started getting restless and bored. See, she'd never lived in the country, and ranching life was all foreign to her. I tried to get her interested and thought if she learned about the livestock and outdoors, she'd come to love it as much as I do. But she had her mind closed to anything and everything about the ranch."

Lynda drummed her fingers against the desktop as she tried to imagine Gideon dealing with such a woman. Frankly, she couldn't picture him in such a situation. Furthermore, she didn't want to think of him being hurt. The way she'd been hurt by Perry all those years ago.

"I don't get it, Gideon. Surely Cecily wasn't blind. She knew you were a rancher and obviously lived on a ranch. What did she think? She could move you away from country life?"

"She had the idea that once I became a lawyer I'd want to move off to a big city. Or, at least, a town much bigger than Tenacity. Once she finally realized I'd never move off Pine Ridge Ranch, she grew distant. And the coming baby only made her more resentful. She wanted to live as a single person, free of the responsibilities of being a wife and mother."

For a moment Lynda remained quiet as Gideon's revelations revolved slowly around in her head. In so many ways, he was describing her, she thought. She definitely couldn't be depicted as being too young to deal with responsibilities. But the remaining-single part fit Lynda to a *T*. She didn't want to be tied down with children and a husband. She wanted to be free to go out and enjoy herself whenever the mood hit her. Not when, or if, she could get her husband off the couch. She didn't want to have to search high and low for a babysitter to watch the kids for a few hours. And then have the babysitter frantically call to summon her back home because one kid had stuck a crayon up the other kid's nostril. No. That was her sisters' married life, and they loved everything about it.

"And after Scotty was born? Did she bond with her baby?" Lynda asked, surprised at how involved she'd become in Gideon's past. She'd never been interested in his private life. Why was she curious now? Something was clearly shifting inside her, and she couldn't blame the weird tilt on invisible cosmic rays. So what was her problem? Was she simply moonstruck?

He said, "No, in fact she started going out more. After a while, I started looking into what she was doing and found out she was with other men. I was hurt, but mostly I was sad for Scotty. Finally, I asked her if she wanted to be a mother to him at all."

"Did she?"

"After we moved into our own house, she made a half-hearted attempt, because she'd made such an issue about getting out from under the watchful eye of my parents. But after a while I could see she was restless and unhappy. By then I realized we were just putting off the inevitable and suggested we divorce. She couldn't leave fast enough."

"How is Cecily with Scotty now? From some of your remarks I've heard you make at work I got the impression you have full custody of your son."

He nodded. "You're right. I do have primary custody of our son. But Cecily does keep him every other weekend. And if she asks to have him on other occasions I let her take him. Where our son is concerned we've worked things out fairly well. She's a more responsible mother now. As for her personal life, I think she has a steady guy, but she hasn't remarried."

"Neither have you," Lynda couldn't help but point out.

He flashed her a smile. "If you're thinking the ordeal with Cecily has put me off marriage, you're wrong. I'm determined to find the right woman and have a good marriage like my parents. It might take me a while to find someone who will be good for me and for Scotty, but I believe I will."

So he was hunting a woman to spend the rest of his life with and to be a mother to his son. Meanwhile Lynda was searching for a guy who could thrill her with a hot kiss. The more Gideon talked, the wider the gap between them grew, she thought. But that was okay. Friends were the most she and Gideon would ever be to each other.

She smiled at him. "I can see you haven't let your failed marriage sour you. And all I can say is you must be a forgiving-and-forgetting person. If I were in your boots I'm not sure I'd be willing to try again," she said, then laughed lightly. "Not that I'd ever try a first time."

But that wasn't exactly true, she thought. She had tried with Perry. And during their romance she'd believed in love and marriage and had trusted his promises to give her both. But nothing about the pledges he'd made to her had been genuine. His deceit had demolished her desire for a husband and family.

He eased into the office chair next to hers. "You like living alone?"

She thought for a moment before she answered, "Most of the time. Why not? I don't have anyone trying to tell me what to do or attempting to run my life. I'm not picking dirty clothes up off the floor—unless they're mine. I don't have to put a pillow over my head to drown out loud snoring or have the television tuned to a sports station twenty-four seven."

"I guess that's one way of putting it. But don't you get lonely?"

Did she? Sure there were times in the darkest part of the night when she didn't like being alone. When she wondered how her life would be in her older years without any family of her own around her. But then she'd think about the men and women who'd come to her office, betrayed and hurt, their lives torn apart by divorce, and she'd feel confident the choice to remain single was the right one for her.

"If I get lonely I go out and socialize. Doesn't matter if I go to Grizzly's or the Tenacity Social Club, I always run into someone I know. Or I go visit my sisters and their kids. And I have a good friend, Ruby, who works as a clerk at Tenacity Inn. She's married to a rancher, Julian Sanchez, and they have two kids. Do you know him?"

He nodded. "I know him but not all that well. A mutual friend introduced us one day at Tenacity Feed and Seed. Since then, I've run into him a few times at the feed store and the vet. Last time I saw him he said he was in the process of building a house."

Lynda nodded. "On the land he's developing into the Start of a New Day Ranch. Right now Ruby and Julian are living in her house on Pine Street, which isn't very far from where I live. But once she and Julian and the kids move to the ranch, I'll have a longer drive to visit them."

"Well, I wish them the best. Ranching is tough work. And I'm not just saying that because I do it."

Strange, she thought. He wore his jeans and boots and hat to work every day, yet she always thought of him as Gideon the lawyer, not the cowboy. But now that he'd talked a bit about his life on Pine Ridge, she was seeing him as that other man, pulling a hot branding iron from the fire, pitching hay and sitting astride a horse. Yes, he'd be more than strong enough to do those tasks. And as she recognized there were sides to him she was only now beginning to see, she realized she wanted to learn more about him. Especially about his life away from the office.

"Sanchez," he repeated the name thoughtfully. "Wasn't that the name of the man who found his fiancée a bit of a ways from here in Mustang Pass after she'd gone missing for a long time?"

"It is. You're thinking of Stanley Sanchez. He's Julian's great-uncle. I'm sure you recall the hullabaloo that went on here in Tenacity a couple of years ago when Winona, his fiancée, was found and her captor arrested. Winona had been kidnapped in Bronco by a deranged man—I think Victor was his name—the day before Winona and Stanley's wedding. For months she had amnesia and believed her captor was her husband. But thank God it all turned out well and Winona and Stanley are happily married now."

"I do remember when it happened, but I didn't keep up with the whole story. When that uproar was going on I was under some heavy stress. Cecily and I hadn't been divorced all that long, and I was taking care of a toddler and learning to be a part of the law firm of Fiske and Jones."

Her gaze slipped slowly over his face, and as her attention lingered on his lips the image of the knight's masked face suddenly flashed in her mind's eye. The image momentarily stunned her, and she closed her eyes against the tempting sight and mentally shook herself.

Now, what was that all about? Gideon wasn't the knight. Could be his lips held a similar shape, but that was hardly a reason to think the two men were one and the same. Actually, the idea of Gideon in a knight-in-shining-armor costume was downright ridiculous. He wasn't the adventurous and playful type.

Confident that she'd gotten her mind back on the right track, she said, "Winona is a mystic. She's been known to help people find their love match. Whenever she and Stanley are in town you should pay her a visit.

She might put you on the right track to find the perfect woman."

His chuckle told him how much stock he placed in a mystic's advice. "First of all, I don't believe in that sort of thing. Secondly, I want to do my own picking and choosing."

Exactly what kind of woman would he choose for a wife? she wondered. Mary once mentioned that she'd seen Gideon's ex in town with their son. She'd described the woman as petite with a short blond bob and a fragile build. Apparently he went for the skinny type. Which definitely left her out. Not that she wanted to be Gideon's type.

She was busy trying to get the image of Gideon and his ex out of her mind, when he suddenly spoke.

"But you have given me an idea, Lynda. You should see Winona and ask for her help in finding your knight in shining armor. She might even be able to conjure up his real identity."

Lynda's jaw dropped as she considered his suggestion, and then in her excitement, she reached over and grabbed his hand. "Gideon, you are a darling! That's a great idea. As soon as I find out when she's in town, I'm going to pay her a visit."

"Lynda, I was only kidding. You're not serious, are you?"

His gaze locked with hers, and instinctively she tightened the hold she had on his hand.

"I'm very serious. About seeing Winona and finding my knight."

"Aren't you taking this whole kissing thing at the masquerade ball to ridiculous lengths?"

His hand was warm, and she could feel a ridge of calluses at the base of his fingers. The same sort of calluses she'd felt on the knight's hand. Had he been a rancher, too? The idea was intriguing.

"I might be guilty of going a little overboard. But it's important to me that I find him. Who knows, Winona might predict he's the perfect man for me."

As his gaze slowly slipped over her face, his hand turned just enough to allow his fingers to wrap around hers, and Lynda was shocked at how intimate the simple contact felt.

"And that will make it so? Lynda, you're a smart woman. It's not like you to go around with these hopeless stars in your eyes."

"Do I have stars in my eyes?" The dreamy sound of her voice warned her that she was headed off to some forbidden place she'd never been before. And she promptly pulled her hand back and cleared her throat. "I, uh, guess I'd better start wearing sunglasses."

He turned his attention to the page of expenditures he'd been studying on the monitor screen and muttered, "Or forget about the knight."

His advice was the last thing she wanted to hear from him. "That's not going to happen," she said crisply.

"You're only looking for a fairy tale, Lynda. Not a real man," he stated flatly.

Except for the boring piped music playing throughout the Dinosaur Center, the room went quiet. Lynda couldn't remember a time she'd ever had a tense moment with Gideon, and this one was making her feel more than uncomfortable. It was making her feel awful.

A couple more minutes passed in silence until Gideon suddenly stood and started toward the door. "Excuse me, Lynda. I'll be back in a few minutes."

Deciding he was probably going to visit the restroom, she was totally surprised when he entered the office later carrying two foam cups of coffee.

"What is this?" she asked.

With a sheepish grin, he placed one of the cups on her desk and kept the other one for himself. "A peace token. I'm sorry, Lynda. I shouldn't have said what I did to you about finding the knight. I realize the effort is important to you, and I was sticking my nose where it didn't belong."

She picked up the coffee and saw it had a dash of cream— exactly the way she liked it—and suddenly she was unexpectedly struck with the urge to burst into tears. He was being nice and apologetic and for some inexplicable reason his sweet behavior was touching something deep in the middle of her chest.

"An apology isn't necessary, Gideon. I'm the one who's sorry for being so short. We're friends. You have a right to stick your nose in my business. And I hope I have the right to stick mine in yours. That is, if I believed I needed to," she added with a half-grin. "It's just that I— I need to find this man. I need to see for myself that there really are white knights and good guys in this rough and tumble world."

He reached over and gave her hand a gentle squeeze, and Lynda had to fight back the tears stinging her eyes.

"I only want you to be happy, Lynda. If you want to have a visit with Winona the psychic, then you should go."

She sniffed and aimed her watery gaze on his face. "Really? Would you go with me?"

From the stunned look on his face, she realized her question caught him off guard.

He sipped his coffee before he finally asked, "Why would you want me to tag along?"

"For moral support. She might tell me something scary."

His smile was indulgent. "Okay. If you decide to have a talk with Winona, I'll go with you."

"Thank you, Gideon. We do make a fine pair—of lawyers. And friends."

"Sure we do."

He turned his attention back to his work, and as Lynda sipped her coffee, she struggled to pull her emotions back together. Which was something she wasn't accustomed to doing. She'd always been a carefree and easygoing person. She'd always looked at the positive aspects of a situation. Except in relationships where she strongly doubted the man's ability to be faithful. And even then, she didn't shed a tear from being angry, or disappointed.

But something had happened to her at the masquerade ball. Now she had to find Mr. Knight, and soon. Otherwise she was going to turn into a woman she didn't recognize.

Chapter Five

Two days later, as Gideon drove Scotty to the school-bus stop at the entrance of Pine Ridge Ranch, he was mentally trying to go over his work schedule for the day without thoughts of Lynda interfering when his son called to him from his child seat in the back seat of the truck.

"Dad, can I go with you to the Dinosaur Center today? You've been promising me. Remember? And I heard you tell Grandma that you get to go there today."

From the moment Scotty had learned his father was doing volunteer work at the center, the boy had been pestering Gideon to let him go along with him. With the weather predicted to be fairly mild for most of the day, he supposed this afternoon was as good a time as any to let Scotty join him at the Dinosaur Center. They'd been making a lot of progress setting up exhibits and activities.

"That's true. I have been promising," Gideon told him. "So, you know what? I think today I'm going to make good on my promise. After lunch, I'll pick you up at the daycare on my way to the Dinosaur Center. How does that sound?"

"Yippee! It sounds great, Dad. Can we dig for bones while we're there?"

Gideon smiled to himself. Scotty was beginning to sound like many of the citizens around Tenacity. Most everyone was excited for the dig to begin. Not necessarily because they were interested in paleontology, but because they viewed the dig as a way to revitalize Tenacity. Whether the dig would be the answer to the town's sagging economy was, in Gideon's opinion, far from a sure thing. But at least the plan gave people hope. And from the looks of the donations that were continuing to filter in, there would be enough funds to get the endeavor started when spring weather arrived.

"No, son. The ground is too frozen right now. And professional diggers will be the people who'll hunt for the dinosaur bones."

"Oh, does that means you and me won't get to dig for bones?"

"Probably not. Regular folks like us don't know what to look for, and we might end up destroying an important bone or fragment."

"Aww shucks, that's no fun," Scotty said with a plaintive groan. "I know what a bone looks like. If I dug one up I wouldn't break it. Buddy digs up bones, and he's not a professional."

Gideon had to laugh at the mention of his father's blue heeler dog they used to herd cattle on the ranch. "Buddy is a professional at burying anything and everything." He glanced over his shoulder at Scotty's disappointed face. "Now that you've found out you can't dig do you still want to go with me? Or would you rather stay at daycare until I finish my work?"

Scotty's mouth dropped open as if he couldn't believe his father's question. "I want to go with you, Dad!"

"Okay. But you should know right now that my coworker, Lynda, will be in the office with me. So that means you'll need to be quiet and polite while we're there. Okay?"

Since Lynda had suggested he bring Scotty one day, he hoped having a child around for a couple of hours wouldn't get on her nerves. Actually, Lynda's opinion of children was something he'd never been able to figure. At times, when she talked about her sisters' children or those of her friend, she sounded as though she enjoyed their company. But on the other hand, he'd overheard her more than once say she didn't want children of her own.

"Okay, Dad. I'll be real good and not make a peep."

"That's my boy," he said.

At the entrance to Pine Ridge Ranch a wide cattleguard made of iron pipe stretched across the gravel road between two matching piers made of native rock. A wooden fence winged out from both piers until it met up with taut barbed wire. To the right side of the entrance a tall, L-shaped pipe held a wooden sign that read *Pine Ridge Ranch, Established 1959.* The year his paternal grandparents poured their hard earned money into the property and built it into a prosperous ranch. Both had passed on a few years ago, but Clem and Wenda Frost were hardly forgotten. A day hardly passed that Gideon didn't think of his grandparents and silently thank them for the ranch and the life they'd passed on to his parents and him.

Gideon parked the truck off the asphalt road the

school bus traveled, then climbed out to help Scotty deal with the straps on the child safety seat and zip him into a red-and-gray puffy nylon coat.

"I don't want to wear my hood, Dad. It's hot on the bus."

"It's not hot out here. The wind is blowing," Gideon reasoned as he tied the hood beneath his son's little chin. "And the bus isn't here yet."

"Yes, it is. I hear it coming."

Gideon straightened to his full height just as the vehicle rumbled to a stop a few feet away and unfolded the door. As he helped Scotty up the steep steps, the driver lifted a hand in greeting to Gideon.

"Hey, Gideon. You ready for some snow?"

Gideon waved back at the older gentleman. "Nah, Ned. Let's hope the snow stays away for a while. We have cows about to drop calves."

"I'll keep my fingers crossed for you, but I hear a storm is coming next week." He reached down and pushed the floor shift into gear. "You tell your dad hello for me."

"Will do," Gideon called to him.

The driver shut the door, and as Gideon watched the bus drive away, his thoughts turned back to the very first day he'd sent Scotty to preschool. He'd not expected to feel a tug of emotion at his son reaching one of the first important milestones in his young life. And Gideon had been caught off guard by the bittersweet pangs he'd felt as he'd watched Scotty going off to learn and mix with other children. Especially when it had struck him that he'd done it alone.

But making a woman a part of their little family just

because Scotty needed a full-time mother wasn't a good idea, he thought as he climbed into his truck. Trying to make a life with someone he wasn't in love with would only make him and everyone else around him miserable.

Last night he and Scotty had eaten dinner with his parents, and afterward, as Gideon had helped his mother clean up the kitchen, she'd kept bringing up the subject of his nonexistent love life. She believed it was well past time for Gideon to start dating again, and his father held the same notion. They wanted to see him with a wife to support and love him. Neither of them stopped to think that finding true, genuine love was not a simple feat.

But Gideon had to admit his single status wasn't going to change unless he started to merge himself back into the dating scene. And the mere thought of being out with a woman, trying to impress her and pretending he was interested, when all the while his thoughts were on an auburn-haired beauty with flashing blue eyes, was downright unbearable.

Face it, Gideon, you're never going to have that family you always wanted. Not as long as you have Lynda on your mind.

Grimacing at the mocking voice in his head, he pressed down on the accelerator. The drive from here to Tenacity took close to thirty minutes. Hopefully in that length of time, he'd have his thoughts cleared.

Lynda limited herself to having breakfast at the Silver Spur Café only on the weekends. Throughout the work week, she normally had a piece of toast or a bowl of cold cereal at home, then finished drinking coffee once she arrived at the office. But this morning, she'd left her house early in order to give herself enough time to stop by the busy café for coffee and to question the waitresses about the masquerade ball and the mystery knight. Unfortunately, none seemed to have a clue to his identity.

Presently, Francine, a middle-aged waitress with a thick waistline and brown hair that was showing two months of gray roots, paused at Lynda's table and tilted a glass carafe over her coffee cup. "I will tell you this, Lynda. There's a stranger in town who's been coming in here every day. The guy never eats, just drinks a soda and goes around asking people about the dinosaur dig."

Lynda frowned. "Really? What does he look like? Or better yet, does he have a deep, gravelly voice?"

Francine snapped her fingers. "Sure does. How did you guess? You know him?"

"No. But I think I know of the person you're talking about. He was at the masquerade ball, too. Dressed like Captain Hook. He came across as Captain Creepy Deluxe."

Francine pointed a knowing finger at Lynda. "Exactly! That must be him."

"Have you learned his name? Or anything about him?"

Francine said, "Not much. To be honest, I got so sick and tired of him questioning people about the dig that I just up and asked him where he came from and what he's doing here."

Lynda wasn't surprised. Francine wasn't the bashful sort, and she'd lived in Tenacity all her life and loved her hometown.

"Did the guy tell you anything?"

"Only that he come from back east and that he was interested in geological digs. Not his name or how long he planned to stick around town. But I'm of the same mind as you, Lynda. He's a creep, and I wish he'd leave."

"If he's spending money around town, then I suppose that's a good thing," Lynda replied. "But I wouldn't trust him as far as I could throw him."

"Same here," Francine said, then gave her a backhanded wave. "I need to check on my other tables. See you later."

"Yes. You take care, Francine."

The waitress moved away, and Lynda thoughtfully picked up her coffee cup and took a sip. Strange that she was able to find Captain Hook's whereabouts, who was a veritable stranger in town, but no one seemed to know or recall anything about the knight in shining armor. Which most likely meant that the man lived nowhere around Tenacity and she'd never see him again. The idea was a bummer, but she couldn't dismiss the probability.

After quickly finishing the coffee, she paid at the front counter and had just stepped onto the sidewalk when a man climbed out of a company truck with his chin tucked against his chest to block the cold wind. As he started toward the entrance of the café, Lynda quickly stepped to one side to move out of his way, while at the same time he looked up and recognized her.

"Lynda! Hey, girl, good to see you this morning. How about having some breakfast with me?"

Grady Bills worked as a lineman for the power company that supplied Tenacity and the surrounding area with electricity. Lynda had known him for years and dated him occasionally. He was a likable guy with a head full of rusty brown hair and a beard to match. He'd been divorced for close to ten years, and Lynda figured it would take a monumental miracle for him to sign another marriage license.

"Thanks for asking, Grady, but I just finished and it's time for me to get to the office. How have you been doing? I've not seen you around in a while."

"I've been good. We're busy, busy with this sudden winter weather. That last storm we had snapped poles and knocked down several lines." He grinned at her. "But that's what I'm paid to do. Fix 'em back."

"You must be doing a great job. I've not lost my power yet this winter."

He made a thumbs-up sign, then slanted her a sly grin. "Say, why don't you and me take a spin over to Bronco next Saturday night? I haven't been on the dance floor in ages."

Dance floor. Her knight. *The* kiss.

The thoughts struck her unexpectedly, followed by the memory of Gideon telling her she needed to forget the knight. Damn it! Any other time, she'd be happy to have a fun date with Grady. Now the idea wasn't the least bit appealing. Not when her mind was on a fleeting kiss and a coworker who was beginning to look like a hot dude instead of a stuffed shirt.

"Uh, thanks for the invitation, Grady, but I'm swamped with work. Call me in a couple of weeks if you'd still like to go. You have my number, don't you?"

Grinning, he patted his gloved hand to the middle of his chest. “Right next to my heart.”

Laughing, she lifted her hand in farewell. “Gotta go. Be careful with those powerlines, Grady.”

She hurried down the sidewalk to her car and quickly drove to the Fiske and Jones office building. As soon as she passed through the cloak room and started down the hallway, she spotted Gideon heading toward his office. This morning he was wearing a dark burgundy shirt with his jeans, and she couldn’t help but notice the broad width of his shoulders and the way his back narrowed down to a trim waist. Had he always looked this good, or was she seeing things that weren’t really there?

“Gideon.”

As soon as she called to him, he paused and waited for her to reach his side.

“Good morning,” he greeted with a smile. “You’re running a little late. I thought maybe you were going to call in sick.”

The fact that he’d noticed her absence surprised her. Gideon mostly minded his own business and left the talking and socializing to the rest of the staff at Fiske and Jones. He’d certainly never appeared to pay Lynda any mind.

“I’m fine. I stopped by the Silver Spur for coffee and talked a bit too long. But I found out something interesting I wanted to tell you.”

His brows rose, and Lynda found her gaze following their arch, then onward to his dark hair. With his hat off, the dark strands waved and flopped onto one side of his forehead and gave him a look that was both adorably boyish and sexy.

"What's that?" he asked.

"Are you acquainted with Francine, one of the waitresses who works at the café?"

He nodded. "I am. She's been there for years."

"Well, she says Captain Hook from the masquerade ball has been coming in, asking lots of nosy questions about the dinosaur dig. She says he's a stranger in town. And even though she asked the man his name, he purposely avoided giving it to her."

"Hmm. How did she know he was Captain Hook? Was she at the ball and danced with him?"

Shaking her head, she said, "Francine didn't go to the ball. But I can assure you if she'd been there, she wouldn't have danced one dance with Captain Hook. No, she and I put two and two together and figured out he's the same man with the same voice. And the same creepy demeanor."

"Oh. Well, did he mention to her why he's in Tenacity? Could be he has folks living here."

"Francine and I know most everyone in this town." She shook her head. "I'll put it this way, Hook would have to be a long lost relative for us not to know him. Anyway, he told her he was interested in geological digs. But I don't think his interest is in dinosaurs. If you ask me, he wouldn't know a hip bone from a neck bone."

Humor twisted his lips. "I'm sure if he's planning some sinister plot against the Dinosaur Center, we'll hear about it."

"Well, I don't trust him," she said flatly.

He leveled a pointed look at her. "While you were at the Silver Spur did you gather any information about Mr. Knight? Or have you quit inquiring about him?"

To make a point, she reached into the pocket of her jacket and pulled out the dinosaur key ring, then dangled it in front of him. "I'm not about to forget Mr. Knight. He stays with me all the time."

A twinkle suddenly appeared in Gideon's brown eyes, and the tiny dancing lights caught her off guard. It was almost like he was flirting with her. Which was crazy. Gideon didn't flirt.

"I'm sure he'd be thrilled if he knew how taken you were with him."

"Are you getting pleasure out of making fun of me?" she asked.

His features suddenly took on a sober expression. "To be honest, I'm actually wondering why a woman like you would feel the need to hang on to a phantom."

She didn't realize her jaw had dropped until she started to speak and she had to pull her lips back together. "What do you mean, a woman like me?"

He glanced over his shoulder to make sure no one else was out in the hallway before he directed his gaze back on her face. "I mean a very attractive woman who has all kinds of men throwing themselves at her feet," he said in a hushed voice. "You don't need a phantom. You have plenty of the real thing."

No, that was where Gideon was wrong, she thought with sudden dawning. She didn't have the real thing. She had make-believe. With herself and the men in her life. But something about Gideon was making her wonder if she truly was wasting her time chasing a fairy tale. He was beginning to make her think she might need more than just a prince with a hot kiss. She might need a genuine, down-to-earth man, who'd always be around to cherish and protect her.

Later that afternoon, as Gideon stopped his truck in the parking lot of the Dinosaur Center, Scotty could hardly contain his excitement. He pressed his nose to the back passenger window and gazed in wonder at the massive flag depicting a life sized image of T. rex erected on the lawn.

"Oh boy! Look at that dinosaur, Dad! He must've been a giant!"

"He's mighty big, all right," Gideon acknowledged his son's remarks. "Ready to go inside?"

"You betcha! But I wanta look at the skeleton in the yard first. Can I?"

"May I," Gideon corrected his grammar, then said, "Sure, you may look T. rex over. Only you're not to touch anything. Just look. And keep your hood on your head. Okay?"

"Okay!"

He helped Scotty out of the truck, then with a light hold on his hand started down the concrete walkway toward the building. When they came abreast of the dinosaur skeleton, Gideon released Scotty's hand and the boy took off in a happy run across the lawn.

"I believe your son is a little excited to be here."

The sound of Lynda's voice had him glancing around to see her walking up to him. She was wearing a red plaid coat with a white scarf draped around her neck. The cold wind had stung her cheeks with a rosy tint and whipped her auburn hair to tangled waves upon her shoulders. The only way he could possibly see her looking any more beautiful, he decided, would be to see her naked body bathed in moonlight. But that was a fantasy with a zero chance of coming true.

Shoving at the erotic picture in his head, he said, "Scotty has been champing at the bit to get out here. But don't worry—I've warned him not to be rowdy while we're here. Hopefully he won't bother you."

She frowned. "Now why would Scotty bother me?"

He shrugged. "Because I know you don't like kids."

Her eyes widened. "I don't? That's news to me. I always believed I loved children."

"You've been quick to say you don't want children of your own."

Her chin lifted. "That's a totally different matter. I love children. I just want to be able to take them back to Mommy and Daddy once my time with them is up. Big difference."

He tried to smile, but his face felt empty. "Yes, a very big difference," he said.

Her blue eyes searched his face. "You look like you're disappointed in me," she said softly.

He shook his head. "No. I'm just trying to understand you."

Laughing lightly, she touched her hand to his. "Best not to try. Sometimes I don't understand myself," she said, then quickly strode across the lawn to where Scotty was gazing up at the huge image of the T. rex skeleton.

Remaining on the sidewalk, Gideon watched in faint amazement as Lynda approached his son. When the boy walked over to her, she squatted on her heels to equal his height. Although Gideon was too far away to hear what she was saying to Scotty, it must have pleased him because he gave her a big grin and shook the hand she offered him.

Deciding it was best to let the two of them interact on their own, Gideon remained on the sidewalk and watched as Lynda joined Scotty in a slow trip around the giant skeleton. Their walk was interrupted at short intervals as she paused to point out certain things about the dinosaur to his child.

When they finally left the skeleton, Scotty was all smiles as he raced over to his father.

"Gosh, Dad, this place is really neat! And Lynda knows all about dinosaurs! She's been reading about them so she can help people understand better when they come to see this stuff!"

Gideon cocked a brow at Lynda. "I didn't know you were actually interested in dinosaurs. I thought you being here was all about getting the town economic help."

"It never hurts to research the subject you're promoting. When people do start arriving for the dig, I don't want to appear ignorant."

She turned her gaze away from him and back down to Scotty's beaming face, and as Gideon studied her lovely profile, he was struck by the fact that he really didn't know this woman he'd worked with for the past two plus years. Yes, he'd seen firsthand that she was a brilliant lawyer in and out of the courtroom. He could also see that she was a free spirit who didn't want anyone trying to clip her wings. She loved to laugh, and she cared deeply about Tenacity and its citizens. But he couldn't quite figure what went on deep down inside her. What was she really thinking and feeling about herself and her future? But on the other hand, understanding Lynda's deepest thoughts wouldn't make him any more attractive to her than he was at this moment. No more than a honeybee to a spoonful of vinegar.

"We'd better get inside," he said, while wrapping a hand over Scotty's shoulder. "The sunshine is nice, but the wind is icy."

"I'm not cold, Dad. Can we look some more outside? At the back of the building?"

"There's nothing back there right now, son. We'd be wasting our time going back there," Gideon told him as the three headed toward the entrance.

"One of these days, I think the people who run the center are planning to make a huge park with lots more dinosaur skeletons and walking trails and picnic areas. It should be fun for everyone," Lynda said to Scotty. "Are you excited about the dig for more bones?"

The boy offered her a toothy grin, and Gideon could see she'd already managed to work her charm on him. Which was quite a feat, considering Scotty was usually slow about warming up to strangers.

"Yeah! But Dad says we can't dig. He says we don't know how to dig for bones. So professionals have to do it. But I have a shovel all my own, and once I cleaned out a whole horse stall by myself," he said proudly, then added, "Well, Dad helped me shovel it into the wheelbarrow. But I did most of it."

"Goodness, you must be really strong," Lynda told him.

"I am. When we get inside I'll show you my muscles."

Lynda looked over at Gideon and winked before she replied to Scotty. "I'll bet your muscles are almost as big as your dad's."

Scotty puffed out his chest. "Almost! But not that big yet. Dad's muscles are big and strong. But I'll be like him one of these days when I grow up."

"I'm sure you will be," Lynda told him.

Scotty looked up at Gideon and grinned, and he could only think how nice it would be if his son had a mother who was around to compliment and encourage him.

The notion suddenly sent his mind wandering to the sweet image of Lynda helping Scotty get ready for school, comforting him when he was hurt or frightened, and tucking him warmly into bed at night. Yes, she would be a good mother, he thought. She just didn't know it yet.

Inside the building, the three of them started up the stairs. While Gideon and Lynda made the climb at a slow and steady pace, Scotty hopped and skipped his way up each step. When they entered their shared office, he went straight to the stack of dinosaur books on one of the lower shelves.

"Is it okay if I look at these?" he asked.

"It's okay," Gideon told him. "Just be careful and don't bend the pages."

He went over to Scotty to make sure the books were

appropriate for him to view. Since he was still too young to read, looking at the pictures was the only enjoyment he could get from the pages.

Once he sat down cross-legged on the floor with one of the books, Gideon started to his desk, when he spotted Lynda entering the room with a folding metal chair.

"I didn't know you'd left," he said. "Where did you find the chair?"

"In a supply room at the end of the landing. There was a folding table there, too," she said. "But I figured Scotty could use a part of one of our desks for a table."

"He's used to sitting on the floor," Gideon told her as he glanced over his shoulder at Scotty, who was already engrossed in the book.

Lynda shook her head. "The floors of this cement building are cold. He might get the sniffles," she told Gideon, then called to Scotty. "Would you like to come sit at my desk, Scotty? I've found you a chair."

Scotty jumped to his feet and, holding the book to his chest, scurried over to the adults. "Is it okay, Dad. Can I sit with Lynda? I won't be loud."

Ruffling the top of his head, Gideon said, "As long as Lynda doesn't mind it's all right with me."

"Of course I don't mind. Scotty is a little gentleman," she said.

Gideon didn't know what to think as he watched her situate Scotty at her desk. This day was turning out to be far different than anything he'd expected. And his feelings toward Lynda seemed to be changing and growing by the minute. Now when he looked at her, he saw a multi-faceted woman. And each side of her tugged at him like the mysterious pull of the moon on the tide.

Later that afternoon, after Gideon and Lynda finished the work that needed their immediate attention, they took Scotty downstairs to the lobby to give him a look at the few geological pieces the museum had put on display so far. As they strolled by a display case with fossil rocks and dinosaur bones that were discovered months ago in the Tenacity area, Lynda was surprised by how much she was enjoying the interchange between Gideon and his son.

Which was rather odd, considering she'd never really thought of Gideon in the role of a father. When he'd first come to work at Fiske and Jones more than two years ago, she'd been told he was a father of a young son. But he'd not talked about his child or any parts of his personal life at all. In those days he'd mostly stuck to himself and, in her opinion, given off the impression that he belonged to a higher social circle than Lynda and her friends. However, she'd gradually learned she'd misjudged him. Little by little, she'd begun to see he was a hardworking rancher who also happened to be a lawyer and that he didn't consider himself to be any better or less than the next person.

And today seeing Gideon and Scotty together was allowing Lynda to see another layer of the man. He obviously loved his son very much and took his fathering role seriously. Furthermore, he was doing most of the parenting. Not an easy task.

When the three of them stopped to study a large oil

painting of a brontosaurus, Scotty tugged on Lynda's hand to catch her attention.

"Lynda, would you be scared if you saw a dinosaur in the yard?" he asked.

Over the top of Scotty's head, Lynda exchanged a knowing smile with Gideon before she answered the boy's question.

"Oh, I'd be terrified," she told him. "I'm not sure what I'd do. Probably call the police and hide under the bed."

Scotty giggled. "I wouldn't. I'd call Dad. 'Cause he can fight off the biggest and meanest animal around! Sometimes he gets on his horse and ropes big bulls and pulls them into the corral! And they have long fat horns that can stab you! But he ain't afraid! He's brave!"

Lynda noticed the boy's brown eyes, which were very much like Gideon's, were shining as they looked up at his father. And it was easy to see the child believed his father could slay any dragon.

Shaking his head, Gideon said, "You know not to say 'ain't,' Scotty."

She gave Gideon a sly wink. "Aw, Dad. Even when he's declaring you his hero?"

To her surprise a blush crept across Gideon's cheeks. "Well, I guess I'll let it slip this time." He reached over and ruffled Scotty's hair. "Thanks for calling me brave, son."

"Is that what you want to do when you get big?" Lynda asked the boy. "Be a cowboy and rope big bulls?"

"Yeah! I wanna ride my pony and brand the calves and all that stuff. And when I get a little older—maybe when I'm six—Grandma is going to teach me how to milk the cow. Right now she's afraid I'll get kicked."

Lynda's questioning gaze went from Gideon down to Scotty's impish grin. "You have a milk cow on your ranch?"

The boy gave her an emphatic nod. "Her name is Cocoa. But she doesn't give chocolate milk. It's just plain, but it's really yummy. And Grandma makes butter from it. She lets me crank the churn. I like doing that."

She looked up at Gideon. "Your mother milks a cow?"

Nodding, he said, "Mom grew up living the country life, and she loves doing outdoor chores. And she doesn't want me or Dad around Cocoa. She says we make the cow nervous, which causes her to give less milk."

Lynda chuckled. "I see. Pine Ridge Ranch must be a busy place. How do you find the time to be a lawyer?"

He shrugged. "Just like plenty of other people who juggle more than one job. But I couldn't do it without my family's help."

Lynda had met Gideon's parents, Joanne and Ash, last year when the staff had thrown a party to celebrate the law firm's twenty-fifth year serving the town of Tenacity. They'd both been quiet, unassuming folks who were unabashedly proud of their son's achievements.

"It's awful how so many townsfolks struggle to make a living," she said thoughtfully. "I have a few friends in the area that hold down two or three jobs to stay afloat. And, unfortunately, some who can't find jobs."

He said, "I know what you mean. My parents have worked hard and struggled just to keep our ranch afloat.

It hasn't always been easy for them. But their love for each other keeps them strong and happy."

Lynda nodded. "My parents are the same way. They've been married for a long time and are still crazy about each other. When they had to sell their house and move away I think I was far more upset than they were. And I realized that the two of them having each other made it easier for my parents to deal with hard times." She smiled at him. "But it would be much nicer if we didn't have hard times in Tenacity."

"I couldn't agree more."

Placing his hand on Scotty's shoulder, he moved the boy on toward the next display, and Lynda followed along. Behind the heavy braided rope cordoning off the exhibits from the visitors stood a four-foot-high pyramid of peridotite and granite rocks, along with some sort of skeleton that resembled a large lizard.

While they stood gazing at the display, Gideon said, "Now that we're working here at the center I'm beginning to catch dinosaur-dig fever. I'm hoping the event will bring in lots of workers and sightseers. And if more bones are actually found, I figure this town will really begin to buzz."

Scotty's little face suddenly scrunched with confusion. "Dad, how do you make a town buzz?"

Lynda laughed loudly while Gideon gave Scotty's shoulders a one-armed hug.

"The town won't actually buzz, Scotty," Gideon explained. "I meant the people will be buzzing with talk about the bones."

"Oh, boy. I'll sure be talking about them. I can't wait

to tell my friend Cody all about this place! He likes dinosaurs, too!"

"Cody is a classmate," Gideon explained to her.

Scotty's enthusiasm brought a smile to her face as she looked at Gideon. "I never knew a little boy who didn't like dinosaurs. And most big boys, too," she added slyly.

Gideon's expression turned a bit guilty. "I confess I never was interested in the creatures before. Not even when they first discovered the bones here during the pumpkin chunking contest. But after working here at the center and listening to your enthusiasm, they're beginning to grow on me."

She didn't understand why, but it filled her with joy to hear she'd had that much of an effect on him. Which was sappy, she supposed. It shouldn't matter whether Gideon was interested in dinosaurs or that he cared about helping the center develop into something profitable for the whole town. But it did matter to her. Very much.

Before she could analyze her feelings too deeply, she reached over and gave his hand a tight squeeze. "Thank you, Gideon."

His gaze caught hers, and the flicker she saw in the brown depths caused her heart to give a hard thump against her breast.

"For what?" he asked.

"For caring about my interests."

Lynda could've told him that never happened to her. But she kept the information to herself. For some inexplicable reason, she didn't want to give him the idea that the men she dated were selfish or uncaring. Because they weren't, she mentally argued. Her dates were simply looking for fun, and there was nothing wrong with that.

Except one of these days you're going to want more than just fun, Lynda. You're going to want someone to care. Really care.

Maybe that's why she'd been so intent on finding her knight in shining armor. She felt sure he'd stepped in to shield her from an unwanted suitor, because he cared about her. And that's really what she'd been searching for all along. Someone to care about her. Not just for a night or a day, but for all time.

The thought drifted through her head at the same time a soft little smile was curving his lips.

"It's my pleasure, Lynda."

The faint but deep sound to his voice reminded her of a seductive whisper, and for a long moment, she found it impossible to tear her gaze from his face.

When had his cute boyish features changed into those of a handsome, caring man, she wondered. When had his brown eyes turned so sexy? And why hadn't she noticed that adorable dimple to the left side of his mouth? The tempting dent had to have been put there just for a woman like her to kiss.

The thought brought her up short, and with a mental groan, she forced her gaze to the exhibit in front of her. This foolish daydreaming about Gideon had to stop, she firmly told herself. They were coworkers, and their bosses forbade fraternizing among the staff. And even if they didn't, Gideon was looking to make a family. Not have a hot affair that would most likely end as abruptly as it started. Besides, something was telling her an affair with Gideon wouldn't be enough to satisfy the longing that had been building in her ever since the night of the masquerade ball. And this one day with Scotty? Was that all she wanted from this precious little boy? She didn't think so.

"Uh, maybe we should move on. This reptile reminds me of a Gila monster. He's scaring me," she said.

Her remark caused Scotty to giggle, and she was greatly relieved for the lighthearted interruption. Not for anything did she want Gideon to get the idea she was starting to crush on him. Because she wasn't.

No. All she was doing was admiring a good-looking guy who was six years younger than her—and her coworker to boot. Damn!

Scotty put a pause on her thoughts as he grabbed her hand and tugged her on toward the next display. "Come on, Lynda. Let's go look at the snake skeletons. They aren't scary."

As Lynda walked along with Scotty's hand holding tightly to hers, she could feel something shifting inside her. And the sensation was far scarier than any poisonous reptile or giant dinosaur. This was a threat from which no dragonslayer could save her.

Or could he?

The question had her gaze drifting over to Gideon, and the slow smile he gave her was like a bright light at the end of a treacherous trail.

Chapter Six

Three days later, snowfall had returned to Tenacity and the surrounding areas. On Pine Ridge Ranch the flakes had been piling up since the early-morning hours. Now, fifteen hours later, snow was still falling as Gideon and his father left the cattle barn to begin the long trudge to the back of the ranch house.

"The drifts are taller than my rubber boots," Gideon commented as they waded their way through the foot-deep snow.

"Yeah, it's going to take awhile for this to melt. I'm glad we managed to herd that bunch of heifers into the barn this morning," Ash commented as they passed through the backyard gate. "I figure ear tag 230, the brown spot, will calve tonight."

"She looked heavy," Gideon agreed. "And something about a storm brings on the babies."

"Change in the barometer, I've always said."

"Good thing we got the heater going in the barn," Gideon replied. "I realize it's an extra expense on utilities, but if it saves a calf or two, we'll be plenty of money ahead."

"Right, son. Saving calves equals saving money."

A light was on over the door, illuminating a part of the screened-in back porch. To the left of the door a stack of fire wood was covered with a green tarp. To the right was a stack of galvanized buckets his mother used for milking, along with several sacks of chicken scratch for the laying hens. On a rubber matt in front of the door, Gideon and his father stomped the snow from their boots before stepping into a long mudroom, where both men quickly shed their heavy coats and changed into their cowboy boots.

"I expect your mother has kept supper warm for us. You're going to stay and eat, aren't you?" Ash asked as he washed his hands at a deep sink situated at the back of the room.

Gideon sidled up to his father and reached for a bar of soap. "I should be getting Scotty home for bed soon. But I guess it would save time to eat Mom's meal instead of making one when we get home."

Ash clapped an affectionate hand on Gideon's shoulder. "I feel guilty about keeping you out so late, son. You should've gone on home and let me handle the ranching chores tonight. You did your fair share early this morning before you headed to town."

"No way, Dad. I don't do enough around here as it is. And you didn't ask for this weather. Anyway, we're in this together, aren't we?"

Ash gave his shoulder another pat. "Always. Unless you get tired of ranching, that is."

Gideon chuckled. "The chance of that happening would be as slim as the moon turning green."

The men entered the warm kitchen to find Joanne

pulling plates of food from the warmer tray in the oven. The scent of lasagna permeated the air, causing Gideon's very hungry stomach to growl at him. A late-morning conference with a client had run much longer than he'd anticipated, and instead of hopping down to the Silver Spur for a regular lunch, he'd been forced to eat a bag of potato chips from the vending machine. Then by mid-afternoon, he'd had to leave for his stint with Lynda at the Dinosaur Center, so he'd made do with a chocolate bar. Since then he'd been running on empty.

"I wondered if you two were going to stay out in the barn all night. Is one of the heifers calving?" Joanne asked.

Swiping a weary hand over his mussed hair, Gideon walked over to the kitchen table and took a seat directly across from his father.

"Not yet," Ash answered his wife. "We've been thawing a water line going to one of the water troughs. And hauling more hay over from the hay barn. But everything was under control when we left."

Joanne placed the plates of food on the kitchen table, then added tall glasses of iced tea. "I hope you don't plan on going back out at midnight to check on the heifers," she said to her husband. "But if you do, you wake me up. I don't want you traipsing around out there by yourself. If you fell and couldn't get back in the house, you'd be a goner and quick."

Ash shook his head, then offered Gideon a knowing grin. "Your mom will never quit being a mother hen."

Gideon looked over at his mother, who was standing at the end of the table twisting the ends of a dish towel until the piece of fabric had turned into a rope. Tonight she looked stressed, which was not the norm for her. But then ranching life wasn't necessarily easy for a woman. Especially if she insisted on doing her fair share of the chores, like his mom. Cecily hadn't been emotionally equipped to handle living in the country, much less capable of doing strenuous chores. And Gideon often caught himself wondering if he'd ever find a wife who could not only deal with living on Pine Ridge Ranch but love it as much as he and Scotty.

"Actually, Dad, I think Mom has a pretty good argument tonight. In fact, if you want the heifers checked in the middle of the night, Scotty and I can spend the night here and I'll go to the barn."

Ash snorted. "Listen, I'm not close to being decrepit. And you could slip on the ice or get kicked in the head just as easily as your old man. So maybe you and I could go together," he relented. "That is, if you don't mind staying over."

Gideon looked at his mother and was relieved to see a tired smile cross her face. "For once, you two are being sensible." She placed a basket of garlic bread on the table, then started out of the room. "I'll go tell Scotty he's spending the night with his grandparents. He'll be happy."

Ash said, "You know, Gideon, your mother would be walking on a cloud if you'd give her more grandkids to spoil. She keeps hinting that it's time you got married again. I try to remind her to keep her nose out of your private life. But she's your mother, and to be honest, I'd be as happy as her if you got married and had more kids to go with Scotty."

Gideon silently groaned. He was bone tired tonight, and his mind was not on hunting a wife. How could it be? All he could think about was Lynda and the sexual tension he could feel sparking between them. Or at least, he knew for certain it was sparking from him. And the looks he'd been getting from her had led him to believe she was far from indifferent to him. Whether they could ever be more than friends, he didn't know. He only knew there was room for just one woman in his mind right now, and that was Lynda. And she wasn't the marrying kind.

"I understand you two want me to have a whole family again," Gideon said to his father. "But that's not as easy as it sounds, Dad. Finding a wife isn't like going to Tenacity Grocery for a loaf of bread."

Ash shoveled up a forkful of lasagna. "I realize that, Gideon. God knows I'd be as lost as a goose if I had to look for a wife in this day and age. But your mother wants you to be happy, that's all. And so do I. Cecily wasn't wife material. But all women aren't like her."

No, Gideon thought. But he seemed to be drawn to the freewheeling sort. What was he anyway? A glutton for punishment?

"Trust me, Dad. I still want to have a wife and more kids. But this time I want to do it right."

"And so you will, Gideon," he said, then reached for his glass of tea. "Now, that's enough about your love life. I wanted to run the idea by you about trading in our open tractor for one with a cab. And yeah, I'm talking a big expense, but it sure would make work nice. Especially when we're mowing the pastures."

Relieved that his father had moved away from the subject of marriage, Gideon began to discuss the pros and cons of the tractor expense. The topic continued until they'd finished eating, and about the time Ash had shoveled up the last of the coconut cake Joanne had baked for dessert, the landline rang with a call for him.

Once his father left the kitchen to go take the call, Gideon rose from the table and carried his dessert plate over to the sink, where his mother was once again tending to dirty dishes.

"Great dinner, Mom. Thanks." To show his appreciation, he lowered his head and pecked a quick kiss on her cheek.

She smiled smugly. "Well, that's probably the last kiss I'll get from you for a while."

The odd statement had him shooting her a puzzled look. "Why? You planning on going somewhere?"

"No. But you are."

Her smug remark caused Gideon to chuckle. "The only place I'm going is to bed, Mom. I'm dog tired."

"I'm not talking about tonight. I mean two nights from now. You're going on a date. Uh—that is—if you're willing to take a lovely young lady out for the evening."

Gideon went stock-still as he stared at his mother in stunned shock. Had someone at the Dinosaur Center said something about him and Lynda looking chummy? No, he thought. That couldn't be. True, there were times they put their heads together over work and times that she touched his hand or arm or he laid a hand on hers. But on the surface, their exchange had continued to remain innocent.

"What are you talking about, Mom? I'm not going on any date! Where did you hear such a thing?"

His question caused a guilty red color to seep into her cheeks, and Gideon suddenly felt very uneasy.

"I've not heard anything. I—"

He interrupted before she could finish, "Mom, please don't tell me you've told some woman I needed a date! If you have, you'll just have to let her know you made a mistake! A bad one!"

Gideon walked back over to the table to collect his dirty utensils, and his mother hurried after him.

"Wait a minute, Gideon. This isn't as bad as it sounds. You know Marisa John, Dawson's wife?"

"Slightly. What does she have to do with this?"

"Well, her sister-in-law, Charity, has been visiting Tenacity fairly often since Dawson married Marisa and moved here. And she's been trying to find someone to take Charity on a date. She's a beautiful young woman and comes from a well to do family over in Bronco."

"Yes, I've heard of the Johns. And I also heard that Charity is beautiful and sings like a bird." Gideon shook his head. "I can't imagine why she'd needed to be fixed up."

Joanne grimaced. "I'm thinking the problem stems from her parents. Marisa says Charity's father runs off every guy who shows any interest in her."

"In other words, she's not met a man with a backbone yet."

Making a palms-up gesture, his mother said, "I think you've hit the nail on the head, son. So you see, it would be nice for her just to go out with someone away from

Bronco and not have to worry about her parents' prying eyes. And who knows, you might enjoy her company."

A big, loud no was on the tip of Gideon's tongue, but suddenly he was thinking about Lynda—again. There was no hope for him to have any sort of meaningful relationship with her. She didn't want to make a commitment to any man, especially him. Maybe it was time he forced himself to move on and try to face reality.

"Maybe so, Mom."

"Does that mean you agree to go?" his mother asked hopefully.

Gideon nodded. "I'll go. When did you say this date is supposed to take place?"

"Two nights from now. I'll confirm the time and let you know when and where to meet her."

At least six months had passed since Gideon had been on a date, and that outing had been so unimpressionable he'd nearly forgotten it. And frankly, he wasn't going to expect much from this date. But if Charity could make him forget about Lynda, even for a half hour, he'd count the outing a success.

"Okay. I'll be ready," he said, trying to sound enthusiastic but failing miserably.

His mother's expression turned regretful as she searched his face. "I thought if you agreed to this date I'd be thrilled. Now I'm a bit ashamed I've done this to you."

"Oh, Mom, it's all okay. Really. I'm not angry with you."

She shrugged. "Well, I know a young man like you doesn't want his mother setting him up on a blind date.

But I—I saw it as an opportunity to get you back into the playing field."

He had to chuckle at her use of words. "A few minutes ago Dad mentioned how much you two would like more grandkids. What is this? A let's-give-Gideon-a-pep-talk-about-marriage night? Sounds like you two have been discussing me."

Her smile was sheepish. "We discuss you quite often. You're our son, and we want you to be happy. If it feels like we're smothering you at times, we're probably guilty," she said, then sighed. "You being our only child—well, it would have been better for all of us if we could've given you brothers and sisters. I guess that's why we want things to be different for little Scotty."

Due to health issues, his mother had never been able to have more children after Gideon was born. She'd never fully gotten over the disappointment of not being able to give her husband more children or Gideon a sibling or two.

He placed a comforting hand on her shoulder. "You're the best, Mom. And just so you know, I want things to be different for Scotty, too. I doubt Charity John will turn out to be the mother of my children. But there's a woman out there who will be, and somehow I'll find her."

Early the next morning, Lynda was in the break room, having coffee with her coworkers when John suddenly looked around the room and then at his watch. "Gideon hasn't made it in yet?"

"No," Mary said. "I imagine he's helping his dad on

the ranch. I heard him say yesterday that the weather was causing a lot of extra work with the livestock."

John grinned cleverly. "Well, from what I hear he's obviously going to find time tomorrow night for some entertainment."

Curious, Lynda asked, "What's happening tomorrow night? Are they having a school play or something?"

With a knowing chuckle, he said, "Nothing so innocuous. I hear Gideon has a date with Charity John. Dawson John's sister, the beautiful young blonde from Bronco."

Mary leaned eagerly forward. "Really? Gideon on a date? What's got into him, I wonder."

Lynda stared at her coworkers, while something inside her chest felt as though it was flash freezing. The sensation was so uncomfortable, she ended up coughing in an effort to ease the feeling.

"Uh, John, where did you hear this? From Gideon?" Lynda asked.

"Hear what?"

All three of them looked around to see Gideon entering the room, like she'd seen him do a hundred times before. Only this time, he looked like a different man to her. He wasn't just a guy with a cute little boy. A guy who never did anything but work as a lawyer and a rancher. Why hadn't she realized before now that there were women who found him attractive? Women who'd be more than willing to go out with him. More importantly, why hadn't she stopped to think he needed and wanted female companionship?

"That you're going out with Charity John tomorrow night," Mary answered Gideon's question.

Gideon rolled his eyes. "Nothing can remain private in this town."

John said, "Well, I didn't know it was supposed to be a secret. I heard it from a waitress at the Social Club. Why? Is it just a rumor?"

"No. It's true."

Gideon didn't look toward Lynda, and frankly she was relieved. Because right at this moment she figured there was a sickish expression on her face. Although she didn't know why. It was none of her business if Gideon went on a date. And yet for some reason it was bothering the hell out of her.

"Well, I hear she's from a mighty rich family," Mary spoke up. "One of the richest in Bronco."

"I wouldn't know about that," Gideon said casually. "Her brother is content to live here in Tenacity instead of on the wealthy John spread. So I figure Charity is just as down-to-earth."

His comment staggered Lynda. What was wrong with him anyway? Had something gone haywire with his common sense?

Lynda and her two friends remained silent as Gideon filled a foam cup with coffee and left the break room. But once he was out of sight, John whistled under his breath.

"Oh man, he's not himself this morning. Wonder what's happened?" He looked at Lynda. "Do you know? You've been working with him at the Dinosaur Center."

Yes, she thought, and their time together had slowly

and surely been working on her emotions. Day by day she'd found herself watching him, gazing at him, thinking how it would be to make love to him. To wake beside him and have him hold her. Like a boyfriend. What an idiot she'd been!

"Listen, I don't know any more about Gideon than you two!" Lynda practically barked. "The guy can date anyone he wants to without asking us for permission!"

Rising from her chair, she tossed the remainder of her coffee into the trash basket and left for her office.

Once she was seated behind her desk, she pulled the dinosaur key chain from her purse and placed the little souvenir next to her mouse pad. But this time as she stared at the trinket, she wasn't thinking about the knight in shining armor and the kiss that had upended her emotions. No, like a fool, she was wondering if Gideon might share that same sort of kiss with the blonde beauty from Bronco.

Charity John turned out to be just as his mother had predicted. She was very pretty and equally nice. She'd even joked about them being set up by their relatives, and Gideon had been grateful to her for easing the initial awkwardness.

Now as they sat in one of the wooden booths in Castillo's Mexican Restaurant, Gideon was trying his best to be an attentive date and keep a pleasant conversation flowing, but as the evening wore on, he was beginning to struggle to keep up the facade. And to make matters worse, Charity could see he was pretending to be interested.

"Are you expecting to see someone here tonight?" she asked.

Her question made him realize he'd been searching the room for a familiar face. Namely one with blue eyes and plump, cherry-colored lips.

"Oh, uh, no. Not exactly. I was only looking around for familiar faces. Tenacity is a small town."

Her smile was a bit indulgent as she reached for a tortilla chip from a basket in the middle of the table. "Yes, I'm fairly acquainted with the size of Tenacity."

A sheepish little laugh slipped out of him. "I guess that sounded stupid, didn't it? Your brother lives here, and from what you say you visit quite often."

"It's a nice change from Bronco," she said pleasantly. "There's a down-home community feel about Tenacity. And everybody seems to know everybody. I like that about this place."

His grunt was full of wry humor. "You need to add that everybody knows everybody's business also."

His comment caused her to laugh softly. "Do they? I haven't noticed a lot of gossiping going on around town."

Shrugging, he said, "Well, that's because I expect you're too nice to listen to any of it."

The front entrance to the restaurant opened, and he looked up from his plate of cheese-stuffed poblano peppers to see if *she* might be walking in. He didn't know why he'd been expecting to see Lynda out and about town tonight. Or why he had Lynda on the brain when he was sitting across from a lovely young woman who was giving him her undivided attention.

Maybe because your brain is permanently stuck on her.

Thankfully, Charity's reply interrupted the mocking voice in his head.

"I'm fairly sure it's that way in every town," she said. "People have their little clans and cliques, and if you're not a part of them you're fodder for gossip."

He nodded in agreement. "Coming from a well-known and wealthy family in Bronco must make you a target for brutal remarks."

Her smile said she was hardly concerned by the notion. "I don't let such things worry me. Of course my parents view things differently. They're all about making grand impressions. And trying to make sure their children don't embarrass them."

"I can't see how you'd ever embarrass your parents."

She waved a dismissive hand through the air. "That's because you don't know them. It's important that people around Bronco put Randall and Mimi John in the same social league as the Taylors and the Abernathys. The two richest families in Bronco," she explained. "So they'd like nothing better than to see me married to someone extremely wealthy."

His short laugh was awkward. "Guess that leaves me out of the running," he attempted to joke.

To his surprise, she reached across the table and gave the top of his hand a reassuring pat. "Relax, Gideon. A woman can tell when a man isn't interested, and it's clear to me your thoughts are with someone else. I'm just wondering why the woman you have on your mind isn't with you right now."

Because Lynda didn't know he was alive, Gideon

thought. Not in a romantic sense. He groaned with misgivings. "Am I that transparent?"

Smiling, she nodded. "I can see it in your eyes. There are moments you slip off to some other place. But it's okay, really."

"I'm sorry. Believe me, it's nothing against you, Charity."

"I understand. And Gideon, whoever this woman might be, she's very lucky to have you. And I'm lucky to have you for a friend. What do you say we shake on it and finish the rest of this delicious meal before it gets cold?"

"I'm all for that," he agreed.

The next morning Gideon had no intention of stopping by the break room on the way to his office. Lynda would be there, and she was the last person he wanted to face right now. Not that he'd done anything wrong. He and Charity had wrapped up the night with another handshake and wishes for each of them to find happiness. No, his reluctance to face Lynda was all about his growing feelings for her. Being with Charity had pointed out just how deeply attached he was becoming to Lynda, and he didn't know how much longer he could keep his feelings hidden from her and everyone around him.

"Hey, Gideon! Come have coffee!" John called to him as he walked by the open doorway of the break room. "Lynda brought pastries, and they're too good to pass up."

Knowing he'd look like a snob if he didn't join them

for a couple of minutes, he turned on his heel and entered the room. He was relieved to see only Mary, John, and Lynda were present. He didn't want anyone else in the office to hear the questions they'd undoubtedly throw at him about his date last night.

"Good morning," he said to the threesome sitting at the table. "Is there any coffee left?"

"The pot has been hit hard this morning," Mary told him. "But I think there should be a cup or two left."

"It's the cold weather," John remarked. "We need something to warm us up. At least the snow has finally stopped. Maybe now I can keep my front steps shoveled clean."

Gideon poured himself a cup of the coffee and sank into a chair next to John and directly across the table from Lynda. Her only response was a faint smile, which was unusual for her. Usually she greeted him and everyone in the office with an enthusiastic *Good morning.*

"There are some raspberry-filled doughnuts left in the box," John told him. "Better get one before they're all eaten."

Gideon said, "Thanks, but I had breakfast before I left the ranch."

Mary's face was lit with curiosity as she leaned eagerly forward. "Okay, Gideon, don't keep us waiting. Tell us all about the date."

"Especially about Charity," John added with a sly wink.

Gideon sipped his coffee, while covertly glancing over at Lynda. She appeared totally indifferent, but Gideon wasn't buying her reaction. She was always interested to hear about other people's love lives. So what was her problem?

He said, "The date couldn't have gone any better. Charity was just as beautiful as everyone had said she'd be. Blonde, petite, big blue eyes, and very classy. I'd say she's just about every man's dream. And to make her even better, she's extremely nice."

Gideon's glowing account of his date put a grin of approval on Mary's face. "You mean she didn't come off as snobbish? And her with all that money?"

"I'd say there isn't a snobbish bone in her body. She was very down-to-earth. All in all we had a very enjoyable evening together."

"Wow! Lucky you, Gideon," John said in a dreamy stupor. "How does a man get a date with a woman like her? It never happens to me."

Gideon chuckled while casting another discreet glance at Lynda. She appeared as though she was in a stupor herself, but it wasn't a dreamy one.

To John he said, "Sometimes you just have to find the courage to ask. You might be surprised. Most women are more receptive than you think."

Although Gideon wasn't sure what kind of response he'd get from Lynda if he asked her for a date. Would she be open to the idea of the two of them together? Or would she tell him to get lost?

"Not to me," John said morosely. "Maybe if I looked like you, Gideon, I'd have a chance."

"Well, tell us more," Mary insisted. "What did you do? Did she sing to you? I've heard her voice sounds like an angel's."

Lynda snorted. “Mary, no one knows what an angel's voice sounds like.”

Mary frowned at her. “I think it would be safe to say an angel's voice is beautiful. What's the matter with you anyway? You need another cup of coffee.”

Lynda looked away from the group of three, who were all eyeing her dubiously. “Sorry,” she said flatly. “I'm sure Charity John sings like a bird.”

This was not Lynda's normal behavior, Gideon thought. As long as he'd known her, she'd never made negative remarks about any woman. If there was ever a champion for the female gender, it was Lynda. So where were these snide remarks coming from?

“I couldn't say whether she does or not. She didn't do any singing,” Gideon told them.

John said, “Well, I'm wondering what you two could've possibly found to do for entertainment in Tenacity. Other than go to the Social Club. I sure can't picture you taking a woman like Charity to Grizzly's for a beer.”

Chuckling under his breath, Gideon said, “Listen you two, I'm not the type to kiss and tell.”

Mary and John both laughed at his evasive answer which seemingly suggested some sort of hanky-panky must have gone on between Gideon and Charity. However, Lynda didn't appear amused. Her lips were pressed into a flat line as she stared at Gideon as if he was someone she'd just met and decided she didn't like.

Clearing his throat, Gideon rose to his feet and with his coffee in hand started out of the room. “See you three later. I need to get to work.”

"Are you sure you have enough strength to make it down the hallway to your office?" Lynda asked.

He leveled a pointed look at her. "I'll manage. But if you think you need to help me, I won't fuss."

"No, thanks," she quipped. "I'm sure if you collapse John will rescue you."

John and Mary both laughed, and Gideon was glad the pair was viewing Lynda's remarks as a joke. Because he could see beneath the too-wide smile on her face that she was being catty. And he wasn't quite sure why. Unless she had something against the John family or Charity herself. But he couldn't imagine that being the case. Lynda hardly ever mentioned anyone from Bronco.

It wasn't until he was in his office taking a seat behind his desk that the thought struck him. Lynda was jealous! As crazy as that sounded, it had to be the reason for her behavior. But why?

Suddenly his mind was going over the past days they'd spent working together at the Dinosaur Center. At times he'd sensed a sexual tension between them, but he'd told himself he had to be imagining things. Lynda wouldn't be attracted to him. They'd worked in the same office building for over two years, and she'd never overtly noticed him before.

Frustrated, he turned on his computer and pulled up a land assessment he needed to work on today, but it took several minutes before he could clear his brain enough to focus on what he was reading. He'd managed to get through one page when he suddenly remembered he needed to make copies of several documents he'd be using at a hearing in the morning.

Grabbing up the documents, he walked down to the copy room and was surprised to find Lynda there, along with a pair of female staff members who worked primarily for Aaron Fiske. As he approached one of the copy machines, Lynda quickly intercepted him.

Her expression was unusually flat as she tapped a folder she was holding against the palm of her empty hand. "I'm glad I caught you here. It saves me from going to your office," she said bluntly. "I'd like for you to look over this land title for me. It's an asset involved in one of my divorce cases, and I want to make sure everything is up and up with it."

He reached for the folder she held out to him. "So one of the ex-spouses wants the land," he stated.

"Of course," she said brittlely. "The husband. The lying, cheating, no-good man! I'm going to make sure the only thing he gets out of this divorce is a boot in the backside!"

Gideon raised an eyebrow at her. "This doesn't sound like you, Lynda."

"What is that supposed to mean?" she asked curtly.

Her dander was clearly up, and the women working at the back of the room must have realized it, because they both walked out.

Gideon said, "I just wasn't expecting you to knock so hard on the husband."

"If the shoe fits," she quipped.

"Yes, but you're all about men and love," he couldn't help but point out.

Her eyes narrowed with speculation. "Love! Don't tell me you've fallen for Miss John after just one date!"

He frowned at her. "I can see right now that Lynda Slater is jealous."

Her mouth dropped open. "Jealous! Of you? No way!"

"Sure!" he retorted. "You're only interested in a random guy you kissed once at the masquerade ball. You're too busy fantasizing about him to notice here's a real guy standing in front of you with real feelings. That's too scary for you to even think about!"

Gideon's words must have hit their mark with her. A parade of stunned emotions crossed her face as she stood silently staring at him. And then, just as she opened her mouth to speak, the door opened and John walked in.

He took one glance in their direction and realized the tension boiling between them. Awkwardly clearing his throat, he strode to the back of the room, and Lynda used the interruption to rush out the door.

Once she was out of sight, Gideon drew in several breaths and tried to calm his rattled senses before he even attempted to use the copier.

John walked up behind him. "What's the matter with Lynda?"

Gideon rubbed a hand across his eyes. She was blind, he thought. That was what her problem was. She couldn't see that he adored her. Or maybe she did see it and wanted no part of him. Either way, it was enough to make him ill. "She's just having a bad morning. That's all."

"Hmm. I've never known Lynda to have anything less than a great morning. Wonder what her problem is?"

"Man problem," he answered with a tinge of sarcasm.

Just not this one, he added.

Thankfully, John went on about his business, and Gideon finished making the copies he needed before making his way back to his office.

Less than thirty minutes later his cell phone pinged with an incoming text. And he stared dumbfounded at Lynda's message.

Can we talk somewhere away from the office?

Quickly, he replied: During lunch break at the library in the back row.

The remainder of Gideon's morning passed in a dazed blur. He wasn't sure what he'd read or written. All he could think about was seeing Lynda. What was this about? Why would she want to talk to him now? She'd left the copy room in a huff.

Once the lunch hour arrived, he drove straight through town to Tenacity Library. Thankfully, Ella McIntyre, the librarian, was busy checking books and didn't notice when he walked in and headed straight to the back wall.

He was standing behind a tall shelf of books, pretending to scan through a book about Montana birdlife, when he caught the sound of light footsteps and looked up to see Lynda hurrying toward him. As usual, she looked beautiful, and as he watched her grow near, he found himself aching for her.

Jamming the book back into the empty slot on the shelf, he waited for her to reach him.

"Lynda, I don't understand. Why—"

She interrupted him with a shake of her head. "Wait, Gideon. Let me explain. I want to apologize for my behavior this morning. You were exactly right. It wasn't like me to be catty—or jealous. But I was, and frankly, it's embarrassing that you and practically the whole office could see it. You're a wonderful guy, and I don't have any business judging who you date."

No longer able to keep his hands to himself, he reached out and wrapped his fingers around her arm. "You don't understand, Lynda. Since we've been working together on the dinosaur project I believe we've grown closer. At least, I know I feel closer to you. I've seen sides of you that I like—very much. And the truth is… I don't want to date anyone—except you," he added softly. "But that's my problem. Not yours."

Her blue eyes were full of misgivings as she gazed up at him. "I happen to think it's *our* problem. You see, Gideon, I haven't been honest with you—or with myself."

"I don't think I understand," he said.

She murmured, "Then I think I'd better show you."

Sliding her hand around the back of his neck, she pulled his head down and fastened her lips over his.

The intimate contact was like a match to an accelerant. Flames exploded and Gideon instantly forgot they were in a public place where anyone might see them.

All he could think was how delicious, how perfect her lips felt moving against his.

Gideon's kiss was all she'd dreamed about and more. The taste and feel of his lips were like sipping a magic tonic. She was floating, dancing on a cloud. Just like the night of the masquerade ball when— Oh no, this wasn't the knight's kiss. She was only having a déjà vu feeling. This was Gideon. A real man, not a phantom.

By the time they finally tore their lips apart to suck in breaths, his arms were wrapped tightly around her and her hands had slipped beneath his jacket and crawled up the front of his shirt where she could feel his heart pounding and the heat of his flesh.

"This is crazy, Lynda!" he mouthed under his breath. "And against company policy, but I don't give a damn!"

She chuckled low in her throat. "I don't give a damn either! Nothing can stop what we're feeling."

He looked at her, and she could see raw hunger in his brown eyes. The same hunger that was building in her, making her whole body hum like an overloaded highline wire.

"No," he said. "But we should probably put a stop to this."

Her brows shot up. "Don't tell me you want to!"

He groaned. "I couldn't stop even if I wanted to," he murmured, then lowered his lips back to hers.

This time their kiss grew even hotter, and Lynda welcomed his hands pushing the front of her jacket aside and the erotic pleasure of them cupping her breasts. His long, lean body felt as hard as a rock against hers, and the heat that was flowing from him into her was like a burst of brilliant sunshine. It felt as glorious as the taste of his kiss, and she didn't want any of it to stop. Not now. Or ever.

A couple of aisles over, Lynda could hear the sound of low voices talking back and forth. The idea of one or more persons stepping around the tall row of books and spotting her and Gideon in a clench should have been enough to make her step away from him. But it was impossible for her to summon that much willpower. Not when the ecstasy she'd been searching for was right here in her arms.

The voices grew a tad closer, and the approaching danger of being caught must've given Gideon a shot of willpower. He abruptly tore his mouth from hers and, with his hands anchored on her shoulders, eased a short distance between them.

"We need to get out of here." His rushed voice was hardly more than a whisper. "Before someone sees us. But I—I don't want to go back to the office. Not yet. Do you?"

Her hands clenched the front of his shirt, as though that was enough to keep the two of them tethered together. "I'd have to be made of iron to go back there now," she answered.

"Then where?"

Her mind darted here and there for a place where they could be alone without being seen, but each place she considered was far too risky. "I can't think of any place—except my house. Do you know where I live?"

"Only the general area."

She quickly rattled off the address, then squeezed his hand. “I’ll leave first. It might be better if you don’t follow directly behind me.”

“I’ll wait a couple of minutes and I’ll meet you there.”

He placed a hot, swift kiss on her lips before she turned and hurried to the front of the building. Thankfully Ella was busy helping someone locate a book on the opposite side of the room and didn’t notice her as she hurried out the door.

Outside the wind felt like it was blowing off sheets of ice, but the chill didn’t begin to cool the fire Gideon had built inside her. How had this happened, she asked herself as she quickly drove out of the library parking lot. After all this time of being near him in the office, why hadn’t she noticed him wanting her? Moreover, why hadn’t she figured out the warm feelings she’d felt toward him were much more than friendship? It was crazy that she’d been so blind and unaware of the spark that had been developing between them.

But one thing she wasn’t blind to now, she thought, as she pressed down hard on the gas pedal. Making love to Gideon was going to be something very different for her. And she needed to make sure she was ready to have her life tilt in a different direction.

What if you’re not ready?

She had to be, she told that voice in her head. Because she didn’t have the mindset or the willpower to turn back now.

Chapter Seven

Something had definitely snapped in Gideon when he'd read Lynda's text asking to meet him outside the office. From that moment on he'd developed some sort of tunnel vision where the only thing he could see was her at the end. It didn't matter if he was blinded to everything else along the way. At this moment nothing else mattered, except getting the woman he'd wanted for so long back into his arms.

How he'd managed to open her eyes to him was a mystery he couldn't begin to unravel. So was the fact that she'd suddenly taken it upon herself to kiss him. But one thing was certain to him: Making love to Lynda was not going to be as it had been with the few women he'd been with in the past. She was definitely all woman and with far more experience in the bedroom than he.

Don't worry about disappointing her in bed, Gideon. This is most likely going to be a one-and-done deal. In a few days she'll realize you want different things in life and move on.

Grimacing at the taunting voice in his head, he turned up the volume to the radio and pressed his boot down harder on the gas pedal. So what if he did mess up and make a fool of himself? At least he could say he tried.

Two minutes later, he turned into the drive to Lynda's house, a modest wood-and-brick structure which thankfully was set back from the street and a fair distance from her neighbor to the left. To the right was an empty field dotted with evergreens. Unless someone just happened to drive by who recognized his truck and knew he and Lynda were both lawyers at Fiske and Jones, then no one should ever put two and two together.

Lynda had parked her car beneath a carport attached to the left side of the house. He stopped his truck directly behind her, and as he climbed out he spotted her standing on the steps next to a side door.

When he joined her, she leaned forward and pressed a kiss on his cheek before grabbing him by the hand.

"This goes into the kitchen," she told him as she pulled him through the open door. "Don't look at the breakfast mess I left on the counter this morning. I was in a hurry."

"I'll keep my eyes shut," he promised as they stepped into the room.

Chuckling, she closed and locked the door behind them, then tugged him into her arms. "Don't worry," she said softly. "I'll lead you wherever you want to go."

Groaning at the thought, he circled his arms around her waist and pulled her tight against him. "I don't care where you lead me," he murmured. "As long as I have you in my arms and your mouth on mine."

Her head fell back, and her blue eyes glittered as she gazed up at him. "You and me—we were not on my radar, Gideon. Why are we just now together? Why have we wasted so much time?"

He slanted her a wry smile. "Because you had your mind on other men, not me. Because I have a child. Because I'm six years younger than you. Because I'm a bit of a stuffed shirt. Because—well, a lot of reasons. But you've been on my radar ever since I first went to work at Fiske and Jones."

Her winged brows made dainty arches above her eyes. "Really? Why didn't you tell me?"

He grunted with wry humor. "I wish I had. But right now, I think we need to, uh, quit wasting time with words. Don't you?"

Her expression turned seductive as she rose onto her tiptoes and mouthed against his lips, "I don't need anymore words. I only need you."

Never in his wildest dreams had he expected to hear her say such a thing to him. And never had he imagined he'd have her shapely body pressed tightly to his or her arms wrapped around him, urging him closer. Altogether, it was causing his senses to shoot off in a million directions. And as his lips crushed down on hers, he could only think his world was changing in this very instant and would never be the same.

In less than a second their kiss turned hot and hungry, and they managed to part only long enough to jerk off their coats and toss them toward the table before they came back together for another long, heated kiss that caused their tongues to mate and teeth to clash.

Red-hot desire was shooting through every molecule of his body, and already he felt as if he might explode any second. When his hand reached beneath the hem of her pencil skirt and glided up her leg, he was desperate to touch her, to connect his body to hers.

Soft and smooth beneath his fingers, her heated skin begged him to continue his upward journey until he reached a barrier of fabric. Urgently, he slid a finger beneath the silky scrap of fabric and touched the moist folds hidden there. She groaned low in her throat, then parted her legs as far as her skirt would allow. He took advantage of the situation by slipping his finger into her warm, velvety womanhood.

The contact caused her to cry out his name as she rocked her hips slowly back and forth against his hand, urging him to go deeper. Her reaction pushed the flames inside him to an even higher height until he felt sure the fiery heat was going to consume him completely.

"Lynda!" he gasped. "I want to give you everything you want. I want to please every part of you."

"Oh, Gideon, you *are* pleasing me," she said, her voice hoarse with desire. "It's perfect! You're perfect!"

Her fingers dug into his shoulders as her mouth latched over his.

Behind his closed eyes, everything turned to a red wall of flames and for one blind moment his mind went blank. He was trying to draw in a breath when she suddenly let out a guttural sound of pleasure, and he realized she'd climaxed before they could ever leave the kitchen.

Burying his face in the curve of her neck, he whispered, "We're just getting started, Lynda."

She gently eased his hand from beneath her skirt, then

with her hand still wrapped around his, she urged him past the table piled with their coats and through a door that entered a hallway. "My bedroom is right down here."

She didn't stop to turn on any lights, and with the shades closed, the room was dim and shadowy. But even if the lights had been blaring he wouldn't have noticed much about the pine furniture or the queen-sized bed covered with an old-fashioned patchwork quilt. All he could think about was getting her naked body next to his.

Once they reached the side of the bed, he pulled her into his arms and locked an urgent kiss over her lips before he moved onto her cheek, then down the side of her neck.

As his lips worked their way downward to her breasts, she was practically tearing at his clothes. He lifted his head, and as they exchanged hungry looks, their efforts to undress turned desperate.

By the time they both fell across the mattress and rolled together, she was still wearing a lacy black bra and his shirt was dangling half off from his shoulders, but neither wanted to waste any more time with clothing. Yet as he gathered her into his arms another thought struck him, and he groaned with frustration.

"Condom," he muttered. "I almost forgot."

Surprise flashed across her face, which told him this wasn't her usual conduct.

"Gideon, you have my head buzzing. I forgot, too."

He had her head buzzing? She had his senses drowning with no chance of coming up for air.

"Don't move. I'll be right back." He climbed off the bed and reached for his jeans.

"You have one with you?" she asked.

The idea that he was prepared for sex clearly surprised her. Frankly, it surprised him, too. He hadn't been with a woman in more than a year, but a couple of days ago, something had made him slip the condom into his wallet.

"I do," he said drolly. "But up until now, it was only for wishful thinking."

She sat up on the side of the bed and watched as he pulled the small square packet from his wallet. "Oh, Gideon. You won't have to just wish anymore. I'll make sure of that."

He slanted her a dry look, and the tender expression on her face touched him in a spot somewhere between his brain and his heart. For a moment, the sensation rattled him. "Can I hold you to that promise? Or were you making a promise?"

"I was. And you can hold more than that—a whole lot more."

Her low, soft voice shivered over him like a whiff of cool breeze skipping across his skin, while the thought of taking her body as his own was almost more than his brain could comprehend.

His hands shook as he opened the condom, and though he tried to calm his trembling fingers, they refused to obey. But his fumbling didn't matter. Suddenly her warm hands were wrapped over his, and their firm hold reassured him she didn't expect him to be perfect.

"Let me do this," she murmured.

A breath whooshed out of him. "I—I'm not sure I can

get through this—you touching me there. You should know—I'm not—some iron man or expert lover."

"No. You're vulnerable and human and that's so much better." She smiled gently up at him. But in spite of that fear, he transferred the condom from his hand into hers. And as she rolled the protective barrier over his hard shaft, he could only think he should be embarrassed to be standing here like this in front of a woman whom he'd only kissed for the first time under a disguise, and only a few more times less than a half hour ago. But this was Lynda and that made everything different. Being here in the broad light of day, revealing his need for her in the most basic way, felt totally natural and right.

When she completed the task, she stood and slipped her arms around his waist. He reacted by wrapping hands over her shoulders and lowering her back to the bed.

Even though one of her legs was hanging off the edge of the mattress, she didn't waste time to reposition herself in the middle of the bed. She urgently tugged him down on her and opened her thighs, and he took advantage of the invitation by entering her with one smooth thrust.

As her body enveloped him, his senses went into erotic overload. He couldn't move or speak or even think as hot desire surged throughout his body and licked at the edges of his brain. If he moved, he feared he was going to splinter into a thousand glowing pieces. But she quickly took that choice away from him, as her hips lifted beneath his and he instinctively followed suit, until he was thrusting deeply into her warm softness.

In the back of his mind, he recognized her hands racing across his back, down to his buttocks, then around to the front of his chest where she rubbed her palms against his flat nipples. Somehow above the noise of his heart pounding in his ears, he managed to hear her murmuring his name over and over as though she'd never spoken it before and liked the way it felt upon her lips.

He dared to look down at her, and the stark desire he saw on her beautiful face was like nothing he'd ever seen or expected to see. Her long auburn hair had loosened from the clip holding it back from her face and now the shiny strands spilled over her shoulders and across one rounded breast. Her moist lips were slightly parted and puffed from the wild kisses they'd shared before they'd ever reached the bed.

He was thinking he had to feel those lips beneath his again, and again when her eyelids suddenly fluttered open and her blue eyes connected to his. The contact was so deep it sent a sharp, sweet pain spiraling through his chest. The sensation robbed his breath.

"Lynda. My Lynda." He breathed her name in wonder before he lowered his head to hers and kissed her.

Her arms clamped around his neck at the same time she managed to snake her legs around his. After that, their need for each other grew to a frenetic pace, and the faster he drove himself into her, the more she asked from him.

Somehow, the melee of their lunges and writhing eventually caused them to end up with Lynda on top of him and her hands pinning his shoulders to the mattress.

"Gideon, I don't want this to end. Tell me we won't leave this room—ever!"

Her hoarse voice made the plea at the same time he realized he was losing all control. He managed to choke out the words "Oh, Lynda—I have to—"

Before he could form the rest of his sentence, he was suddenly flying weightless and tumbling out of control to a place he'd never been before. The journey was filled with a kaleidoscope of whirling colors blinding him with their brilliant beauty.

Somewhere along the way, he heard her loud moan and then her damp body collapsing over his. At that moment, the desire to lift his arms and wrap them around her was all he wanted, but he was too dazed and exhausted to make his limbs move.

Eventually, he managed to weave his fingers into a thick wave of her hair. While he stroked its silkiness, he drew in ragged breaths and tried to calm his runaway heart.

Finally Lynda began to stir, and he closed his eyes and soaked in the pleasure of her hand gliding up the side of his ribcage and down his arm. "You were incredible, Gideon. Thank you."

He tried to chuckle, but the sound came out more like a painful grunt. "Incredible? You don't have to spread it on, Lynda. My ego isn't all that important to me."

She scooted up his chest and rubbed her cheek against his. "You never need to worry about ego, Gideon. You're a good man." She kissed one cheek, while trailing her fingers gently against the side of his face. "That's why I thought I'd never have you here with me like this."

He frowned. "Why? What does that mean?"

Her mouth curved into a rueful smile as she lifted her head and looked at him. "Nothing—except—well, I've been so intent on searching for the knight I kissed at the masquerade ball because I wanted to find a good man and I believe he is one. But now I have you in my arms, Gideon, and you're a good man. Very good," she murmured. "But now I'm afraid we've both run well over our lunch hour. So how are we going to handle this when we get back to the office?"

Groaning with misgivings, he gently eased her back far enough to allow him to sit up on the side of the bed. "I don't know. Do you have any ideas? That we had to go check on some papers that needed signatures at the Dinosaur Center?"

"And what if someone called out there to check just to see if we were there?" she asked.

"Who would do such a thing? Certainly not John or Mary," he said.

"No. But we might get caught up in the fib. Why don't we just tell the truth," she suggested.

"The truth!" The words burst out of him. "That the two of us couldn't get back to work because we were too busy having hot sex?"

Her wicked laugh made him want to push her back down on the mattress and go for a second round.

She said, "That wasn't hot sex, Gideon—what we had was *torrid* sex!"

Afraid he was going to give in to the urges returning to his body, he reached to the floor for his jeans. "Hot or torrid, the truth is off the table."

"When I said 'truth,' I meant something like…neither one of us was paying attention to the time," she explained. "Which is true—up to a point."

He grimaced as he zipped his jeans. "You sound just like a lawyer."

"I am a lawyer," she reasoned. "We both know how to fudge the truth."

"I don't like lying," he quipped. "It's not good."

She pulled on her panties, then stepped into her skirt. "Neither is being fired for fraternizing with another lawyer in the firm."

While he stuffed his shirttail into the waistband of his jeans, he tried to read the expressions on her face. "Okay. I'll find another job somewhere else. I'll have to commute a long distance, but I can manage."

Shocked by his suggestion, she stared at him. "Quit being ridiculous! I'm not about to let you quit Fiske and Jones. Not for me!"

"Why? Because this—you and me—it's not important to you?"

Her lips parted as her face went pale, and he realized she'd not been expecting such a pointed question from him. Maybe the men she'd had in her life before now hadn't cared enough to ask it. Or they were smarter than Gideon and knew she wasn't in the market for anything serious. But damn it, a few moments ago, when she'd been in his arms with their bodies locked in heated passion, she'd felt very serious to him. Was he so much of a fool he couldn't see through a woman's kiss?

"Gideon." She said his name softly as she stepped over to him. "You've misunderstood me. I only meant that your job is important. Aaron and Basil put a high value on your work. And I know you're proud of your position with them. This thing with you and me—it's all new and just beginning. I don't think either of us should make any life-altering changes in our lives until—well, later."

In other words, after they saw if a relationship between them was going to work, he thought dismally. Well, he wasn't going to push her for more. Not now. Like she'd said, things were just beginning with them. He didn't want to pressure her or have her thinking he might turn out to be a possessive partner who'd barely give her enough space to breathe.

Glancing away from her, he drew in a ragged breath. "Yeah. You're right. We should, uh, take things slowly. And see how things go."

Moving closer, she slipped her arms around his waist and pressed her cheek against his chest. The tender gesture caught him by surprise and so did the bittersweet pain that followed.

"Gideon, you've always been so much of a gentleman and treated me with kindness. You make me feel like a princess who deserves the best. I've never felt that way with any man until you. And now, being here with you like this… It's been special for me. Now, when we're at the office it's going to be a struggle to look at you and pretend I don't want you. Because I will be wanting you. Probably more than you know."

Emotions suddenly came out of nowhere to create a thick lump in his throat. He tried to swallow it away, but his voice still sounded strangely hoarse when he spoke. "I've been looking at you and wanting you for a long time. But after this, it's going to be hell not to touch you."

Lifting her head, she gazed up at him, and this time her blue eyes were soft and promising. "It will be worth it, Gideon. Especially when we focus on being together again—away from the office."

"Together again," he repeated, then because he couldn't stop himself he lowered his head and placed a long kiss on her lips.

By the time he made himself pull away from her, he was aching to make love to her again, and if the clamp of her arms around his waist was anything to go by, she was feeling the same.

Clearing his throat, he eased away from her. "We'd better get going. I'm parked behind you, so I need to leave first."

She found her red high heels at the foot of the bed and quickly jammed her feet into the shoes. "Okay," she said. "I have to redo my makeup, but I'll be there shortly."

"If anyone asks, I've not seen you," he said.

She chuckled under her breath, then blew him a kiss. "Right. We've not seen each other since this morning before lunch."

Later that afternoon, Lynda was back at work, making last-minute notes for a court appearance with a client, when it struck her that she'd made a terrible mistake by going to bed with Gideon.

When she'd kissed him in the library, the connection

had been instant combustion and she'd been blown away at how perfect it had felt to be wrapped in his embrace with his lips devouring hers. And all she'd been able to think about was having sex with the hunky young cowboy lawyer. Sure, a part of her had told her that sex with Gideon wouldn't be the same experience as with the partners she'd had in the past. He was a proper sort of guy, and she'd thought he'd be the same in bed—cool and perfunctory. She'd thought it would be nice and enjoyable. Never in her wildest imaginings had she expected their union to be an earthquake that would shake up every indifferent attitude she'd ever had about men.

Now she didn't know what to think or how she was going to deal with these newfound feelings Gideon had evoked in her. He'd not only made her crazy with desire, he filled her with a sense of tender belonging. After they'd made love, she'd wanted to curl up against him, to hear his heart beating and feel his breath brush her cheek. She wanted more time with him. Time to explore every inch of his body and learn his innermost thoughts.

There were so many aspects about him that she admired. His devotion to Scotty and the respect he had for his parents. His ambition to be a good lawyer for the firm and the extra hard work he put in to help the Frost family ranch stay afloat. There were also sides of him she wanted him to share with her. Like his deepest wishes. Not only for himself, but for Scotty, too. She wanted him to tell her about all the things he considered important in his life.

And yet, even without knowing Gideon's innermost thoughts, she knew without a doubt he was a good guy—just the sort of princely knight she'd been searching for. Odd, she thought, how these past weeks she'd been on a search for her white knight, the only thing on her mind had been locating him. Never once had she really thought about what might happen if she did actually find him.

These strange reactions and thoughts she was having about Gideon were crazy. She'd never once felt or wanted such things with another man. So why was it all so different with Gideon? And why, before she left her bedroom this afternoon, did emotional tears burn her eyes? She was behaving like a sentimental woman and it was scaring the crap out of her.

If she was smart and wanted to put her common sense on display, she'd tell him there couldn't be anything else between them. He needed to find himself a nice woman looking for a husband, one who wanted to be a ready-made mother. Not a woman like her, who'd built thick steel walls around her heart so she'd never be vulnerable again. But somehow Gideon had gotten in. And now she was vulnerable. Because for the first time in her life, he'd made her feel loved. How did a woman give that up?

Once Lynda entered the courtroom later that afternoon, her professional training took over and she managed to push Gideon and all that had happened between them to the back of her mind. She was triumphant when the judge ruled in her client's favor and returned to the office feeling good about her work. Yet as soon as she returned to the Fiske and Jones building and walked down the hallway to her office, everything inside of her wanted to keep walking until she reached Gideon's door. For some inexplicable reason she needed to see his smile, hear his voice.

Sighing, she made herself enter her office. There was a stack of work waiting on her desk. She didn't have time for dreaming.

Five minutes later, she was reading through notes she'd taken from a recent client when a knock sounded on the door.

Not bothering to look up from the typewritten notes, she called, "Come in."

"It's me, Lynda."

The sound of Gideon's voice caused her head to jerk straight up. "What are you doing?" she asked in a loud whisper. "We can't—"

Grinning, he walked over to her desk. "Calm down. I'm not here for a quickie. You ought to know I'm not that reckless. Even though I'd like to be."

A pent-up breath rushed out of her. "Oh. I was just thinking about you—and us," she admitted.

A pleased look crossed his face. "You've given me hope."

Hope for what? she wondered. For a future with her? Or simply for a few more sessions of sex? The questions were steamrolling through her mind, but she wasn't about to ask either one of them. Right now she needed to slow this thing between them before it roared completely out of control.

Clearing her throat, she said, "Then why are you here? To tell me Aaron and Basil noticed we were late getting back from lunch?"

"No. When I got back here, neither man was in his office. So we're in the clear. Unless someone wants to make an issue about it," he said, then went on: "I wanted to let you know I just got a call from the Dinosaur Center. Later this afternoon workers are going to be servicing some of the electrical wiring in the building, so they'll be cutting the power. We'll have to forgo our volunteer work for today."

Disappointment washed through her. "Oh, I was looking forward to us going out there. I realize the office where we work is practically a wall of windows, and it's not like we'd have a chance to, uh, really be together. But at least we'd be sitting next to each other without anyone else around."

She sounded like a teenager eager to hold hands with her steady date, but she didn't care if she was being ridiculous. Something about Gideon was making her feel young and happy. What could be so wrong with that?

"I know. I was thinking the same thing. They said the power will be back on tomorrow and the elevator should be in working order. We can get back to our charity work then. Other than that, I—"

"Can you come to town tonight?" she interrupted with the question.

He shook his head. "Afraid not. Dad wants me to go with him to check on some cows that were snowed in on the far back side of the ranch, and we promised Scotty he could go with us. I can't let both of them down."

"Of course you can't," she said, while reminding herself the man had responsibilities. She understood he had a ranch to help run and a young child who needed his care and attention. But where did that leave her? Moreover, did she want to be a part of Gideon's commitments? "I was only wondering when we might be able to get together again."

He glanced at the closed door before reaching down and touching his hand to hers. "Believe me, Lynda, I'm wondering the same thing. Tomorrow is Friday. I might be able to get away from the ranch for a while on Saturday. We'll talk about it at the Dinosaur Center tomorrow afternoon. Okay?"

Nodding, she gave him the most understanding smile she could muster. "Okay. But I'll think about you tonight."

The hungry look on his face made something inside her actually hurt. Did that mean she was already gone on the man? No, she was only feeling disappointment because she had to wait to be with him again. That was where the pain was coming from, she tried to reason with herself.

"I'll think about you, too," he told her, then before she could say more, he turned and strode out of the office.

Once the door shut behind him, Lynda flopped weakly against the back of her chair. She had to get a grip. She had to recognize that Gideon was no different from any other man who had come and gone in her life. This deep longing she felt for him would soon die a swift death, and then she could go back to being the emotionally untouchable woman she'd sworn to be some ten years ago.

Chapter Eight

"How are things going at Fiske and Jones, son? Everything okay?"

Gideon looked over at his father as the old work truck rumbled over a dim track across wide open pastureland. Although it was dark and once again snow had begun to fall heavily, the vehicle's headlights were enough to show a dark line of woods in the far distance. Both Gideon and his father expected the cattle to be sheltering there beneath the thick stand of ponderosa pines and Douglas firs.

"Sure, Dad. Everything is going fine. I've got enough work to keep me busy."

"Yeah, I guess businesses in town are always changing hands, same with rural property around here. People buy into it with the idea they can make a go of ranching or farming. Most of them are clueless to the cost and labor that goes into raising crops or livestock. Unfortunately, they end up going broke and forced to sell out. And then, too, there are the older folks who aren't able to take care of a farm or ranch any longer."

Gideon could hear a faint wistful note in his father's voice, and the sound caught him by surprise. Ash Frost never considered himself too old to do anything. And Gideon had always expected his father would have that same attitude even after he entered his eighties, which was still decades away.

"What's the matter with you, Dad? You're still a young man. You sound like you're not too far away from retirement. You're not thinking about sitting down on the job, are you?"

Ash frowned at him. "Heck no. I have lots of years left in me, God willing. I guess I was just thinking about the future. One day you'll have to take over the reins of Pine Ridge Ranch, but I won't regret that. 'Cause I know this place will be in good hands."

"Don't worry, Dad. I want this ranch to be just as productive when I have to turn it over to Scotty someday," Gideon assured his father.

"Dad, when are we gonna see the cows? Did they all run off?" Scotty asked from the back seat, where he was strapped tightly beneath a seat belt.

Gideon glanced over his shoulder at his son. He was bundled up in a scruffy brown coat that Gideon had long ago determined a play coat. A red sock cap was pulled over his ears and down on his forehead. The boy was always excited to tag along on special outdoor chores, and Gideon could only hope his son's enthusiasm in the ranch would remain once he grew into adulthood.

"Hang on, Scotty. We'll be there in another minute or two," Gideon assured him.

Normally, they'd have ridden their horses out to check on the little herd. But given the limited daylight and the icy precipitation, they'd been forced to climb into the old work truck. Which, next to a horse, was Scotty's favorite mode of transportation.

"I wanna see Bernie," Scotty said. "He has big long horns—just like I told Lynda. I bet she'd like to see him, too."

"I'm not sure Lynda likes bulls. She might be scared to get close to one," Gideon told him, while trying to imagine Lynda in this dusty old truck bouncing over a rough trail. As far as he knew, she'd never been a country girl. But that didn't mean she would frown on living on a ranch, away from the lights of town. Not that Tenacity was an exciting metropolis, but compared to Pine Ridge Ranch it was a lively place.

"When can we see Lynda again, Dad?"

Gideon stifled a sigh. "I don't know, son."

"Why don't she come out here to the ranch?" Scotty persisted. "'Cause you ain't asked her?"

"Don't say 'ain't,' Scotty. And no, I haven't asked her."

"Who's Lynda?" Ash wanted to know.

Scotty was quick to answer. "She's really pretty, Grandpa. She smells really good, too. And I like her. She taught me a whole lot of stuff about dinosaurs."

No doubt Scotty had been totally charmed by Lynda. Close to a week had passed since the boy had visited the Dinosaur Center and she'd given him her undivided attention. He was still talking about her and asking to see her again. Gideon was pleased that she'd bonded with his son. Even so, that didn't keep him from worrying over the fact. No one had to tell him that Lynda was like a bird; she might decide to take flight at any given moment. Whenever that happened, he didn't want Scotty to be hurt.

"He's talking about Lynda Slater," Gideon explained to his father. "She's a fellow lawyer at Fiske and Jones. And a friend. I think you and Mom met her briefly last year at the Fiske and Jones twenty-fifth-anniversary party. Auburn hair…a little older than me."

"Oh yes, I remember. And you consider her just a friend?" Ash asked slyly.

Gideon didn't want to lie to his father, but considering the circumstances, it might not be wise to tell the complete truth. At least, not yet. Not until he and Lynda decided exactly what they were together.

Gideon said, "Well, friends are all we can be, Dad. Fiske and Jones has a policy that the employees can't fraternize."

"I see." He shot Gideon a suggestive grin. "That must make things a little tough."

"Why?"

Ash chuckled knowingly. "Like Scotty said, she's pretty and she smells good. Kinda hard to resist, huh?"

Resist? His father couldn't begin to guess the half of it. Gideon had failed miserably at resisting Lynda.

"Okay, I, uh, do wish the two of us could be more than friends. But I can't see how it can happen. Or even if it would work."

"I figure you'll find a way to make it work," Ash said. "If you want it to."

Gideon let out a long breath. "I don't want to make another mistake, Dad. The first one I made was bad enough."

Ash reached over and poked a finger in the middle of Gideon's chest. "Just follow what's in there and you'll be fine."

In other words, ignore what was in his head, or in his jeans, Gideon thought wryly. But didn't his father understand a man's heart was his most vulnerable part?

"I'll try to remember that, Dad," he said, then gestured to the tree line up ahead. "I see the cows. They've heard the truck coming."

"Can I get out and help?" Scotty asked eagerly. "I can toss hay."

"I suppose," Gideon told him. "But you have to stay right by my side. And if Bernie comes close, don't try to pet him. He'll hurt you."

"But he's not mean. He's nice."

"You're right—he's not mean. But he might hurt you without meaning to."

Just like Lynda might hurt Gideon without meaning to. But why was he worrying about getting hurt now? He should have been worried about that before he'd had—what had she called it?—*torrid* sex with her.

Thankfully, Gideon's worrisome thoughts were interrupted as his father braked the truck to a halt and gave the horn a couple of blasts to make sure all the cattle would hear and come running for their feed.

"There's the cattle," Ash announced. "Let's get to work so we can get back home and eat our supper."

When Lynda arrived home after work, she didn't bother getting out of the car. Instead, she called her friend Ruby to see if she was home and could deal with thirty minutes of company. Luckily, Julian was busy working on the home he was building for them out at the ranch, so Lynda didn't feel all that guilty about barging in on her friend.

She entered Ruby's house by way of the kitchen and found her busy cooking the evening meal. Dressed in worn jeans and a faded red sweatshirt, she looked tired but utterly content.

"Hi, stranger," Ruby said with a happy grin for her friend, then eyed Lynda's pencil skirt and blazer. "What's this? You haven't been home to change clothes?"

"I didn't take the time." She gave Ruby a hug, then walked over to the kitchen table and sank into one of the wooden chairs. "I'm sorry, Ruby. I know you're terribly busy, but I need to talk. I called my sisters before I left work this evening, to see if one of them would be my sounding board, but they're both tied up with school functions," Lynda told her.

"Since when do you need to apologize for dropping in for a chat?" Ruby scolded.

"Maybe since I've been thinking about all the work it takes to be a wife and mother." She glanced toward the door leading into the other part of the house. "Where's the kiddos?"

"Emery is watching one of her favorite cartoons on TV, but if she hears you in here, watch out. She'll be in your lap."

Lynda said, "Like that would bother me. Emery is a little darling. And what about Jay?"

"Napping in his crib. I have the intercom on so I'll

hear him if he stirs." She gestured to the coffee maker at the end of the cabinet. "Like a cup of coffee?"

"If you have it made." She jumped up from the chair. "I'll get it myself. You tend to whatever you're cooking. By the way, it smells delicious. What is it?"

"Swiss steak." She pointed the wooden spoon she'd been holding at Lynda. "And before you say anything, yes, I know, no one makes Swiss steak anymore, except me. But Julian loves the dish and it makes me happy to make him happy."

Lynda filled a cup with coffee and added powdered creamer. "I'm glad you're happy, Ruby. No one deserves it more than you."

"Oh, I wouldn't say that. Everyone deserves a little happiness in his life." She shooed Lynda toward the table. "Go sit. I'll get a cup and join you. The meat is simmering now. It'll take care of itself."

After Ruby had joined her at the table, Lynda said, "I guess you're wondering what I want to talk about."

"I don't have to wonder. From the looks of you, it's got to be a man."

"Is it really that obvious?"

Ruby gave her a look.

"Okay. I won't try to deny it. But Ruby—" She paused and shook her head. "This is like nothing that's ever happened to me before. And it's scary!"

Ruby's mouth dropped open. "Don't tell me you've found the knight in shining armor? The one with the mind-blowing kiss?"

For a moment Lynda could only stare at her blankly. "Oh, I—no. I haven't found the knight. I haven't even been looking for him. In fact, I'd forgotten all about him."

"You must be joking. You were carrying on about the guy like finding him was a matter of life and death. How did you go from that much urgency to forgetting the man?"

Lynda rarely blushed, but right now she could feel heat blossoming on her cheeks. "All right, I admit I sound like a fool. And that's probably what I need to hear from you. For you to tell me I'm behaving stupidly."

Lynda rolled her eyes. "How can I tell you're behaving stupidly when I don't know what you've been doing—yet."

Lynda sipped her coffee before she sucked in a bracing breath. "Okay, I've had sex with the wrong man."

Unflinching at this news, Ruby asked, "So what makes him wrong?"

"Several things. First of all, he's a family man, a single father with a four-year-old son. Secondly, he's six years younger than me. And thirdly, he's also a lawyer at Fiske and Jones. Which, according to the firm, means seeing him on a personal basis is a no-no."

"Oh, is that all? And is there a fourthly? Or is there such a thing as a fourthly?"

"Actually, I think there is such a thing. And there probably is a fourthly—like he makes me feel over the moon! Completely and utterly flying from star to star. I've never experienced anything like him, Ruby! And it's all so shocking! All along I thought he was the next thing to a monk. He's a very upstanding kind of guy. I never once pictured him being a red hot lover."

Shaking her head, Ruby reached for her coffee. "I don't understand, Lynda. What's wrong with a red-hot lover? You should be thrilled. Even though it sounds as though you're going to have to sneak around to stay out of trouble with Fiske and Jones."

Lynda swallowed and looked away from her. "You're right, Ruby. What woman doesn't want to be thrilled when she's in bed with a man?"

"A woman who goes to bed to get some sleep, I suppose."

Lynda groaned and laughed at the same time. "Well, in this case, I'm not talking about sleeping."

"Exactly what is it that has you running scared?" Ruby asked. "Are you worried you might actually start caring for this guy?"

Lynda felt the ridiculous urge to burst out bawling. "Oh, Ruby, Gideon makes me feel things I don't want to feel. He touches me in spots that have nothing to do with my body. I don't know what to think—except that I'm headed for trouble."

Ruby studied her for long moments before a wide smile spread across her face. "But why? Oh, honey, this is the most wonderful thing that could happen to you! A man, a decent man at that, has finally broken through that tough hide you've wrapped around your heart. Now you're going to discover what it means to care about a man—to want to share your life with him."

Frowning, Lynda said, "But Ruby, all of that is exactly what I don't want. Why should I want to share my life with just one man? Why tie my hands with motherhood? The way I am now I can do whatever, whenever. What kind of fool would want to give that up?"

"A fool in love," Ruby answered, then added with another roll of her eyes. "Oh, but I forgot. You're the woman who doesn't ever want to fall in love."

"Ever? Well, I wouldn't go so far as to say *ever*. Maybe when I get in my forties and find the courage to risk my heart I might get the urge to settle down."

Ruby shot her a tired look. "Sorry, Lynda, that's not the way love works. You don't pick and choose a time for it to happen. When you're hit with the real thing, it clamps on and won't let go. No matter how hard you fight against it, or how many thick walls you try to build around your heart."

Lynda had been fighting all right. Ever since she'd walked out of her house after making love to Gideon, she'd been struggling to push aside the tender feelings that had unexpectedly assaulted her. For all these years, she'd believed she'd hardened her emotions enough to make them impenetrable. Now, she wasn't so sure. But it was too early to worry about really falling for Gideon, she argued with herself. Or was it?

"Well, thanks, Ruby, for being so reassuring," she said with sarcasm. "You've given me such peace of mind."

Laughing now, Ruby reached over and gave Lynda's hand a squeeze. "Relax. I promise you're going to survive this. So how did this thing with Gideon happen? What made you two get together after all this time?"

"What do you mean 'after all this time'?"

"Excuse me, but didn't you tell me that Gideon also worked at Fiske and Jones?"

"I did. He's been there for more than two years."

"That's my whole point. Why did it take so long for you two to get together?" Ruby wanted to know.

Shrugging, Lynda took another sip of coffee. "Oh, I had always noticed he was nice, but my thoughts never went any further. But then Basil asked the two of us to do charity work together out at the Dinosaur Center, and that drew us up close and personal. I don't know what happened, Ruby. I just began to notice him as a man. And you know what—he told me that he'd noticed me from the very start. I didn't have a clue."

"Why not? *Every* man notices you, Lynda."

Lynda groaned. "Not really. And now I wonder if Gideon's attraction for me is a good thing. He's a family man, Ruby. He even lives on the family ranch. Not with his parents—he has his own house, but fairly close by, I think. And I'm fairly sure he wants more children."

"He's said this to you?"

"Not exactly as straightforward as that, but that's the impression I get from him. Which is understandable. He's only twenty-seven and having a family is important to him. See, he's an only child and I don't believe he wants Scotty to go through life without a sibling or two."

"So children are important to him, but not to you," Ruby said.

"Look, Ruby, you know as well as anyone that I've always loved children. It's not that I'm against being a mother. It's just that being a mother means committing myself to a man and exposing my heart to him and the kids. If things didn't work out with him…if he walked out on me…it wouldn't be only me suffering. Our children would suffer, too. Maybe I could risk being a wife, but I'd hate to risk a child's happiness."

Sighing, Ruby said, "Yes, I'm living proof that marriage and motherhood is a gamble with your heart. But when things go right, Lynda, the whole world is a beautiful and better place."

Motherhood. Lynda's mind latched on to Ruby's one word as her thoughts turned to Scotty. She'd not expected to enjoy the little boy as much as she had when he'd visited the Dinosaur Center. She'd not imagined she could have such strong maternal feelings and she'd been surprised at how much she'd wanted to hug him close and hear his happy giggles. And when she'd told the child good-bye that day, she'd not wanted to consider the possibility it would be the one and only time she'd see him. What had those unexpected feelings mean? That deep down she longed to be a mother?

Swallowing at the ball of emotion in her throat, she said, "I'm glad it's worked out that way for you, Ruby. But I'm just not sure I'm brave enough to become a wife and mother."

Shaking her head, Ruby said, "Well, my only advice is to go on seeing Gideon. And if you begin to feel like you're getting emotionally attached to the guy and you want to end things with him, then all you'll have to do is tell him goodbye."

End things? Sure, ending things with a man had always been easy for Lynda. But now? She couldn't picture herself telling Gideon it was all over. It was impossible for her to imagine not talking with him, kissing and making love to him. Or even worse, imagining him sharing his life with some other woman. Like Charity John. So what did that mean?

Two days later, after a long session of afternoon lovemaking, Gideon and Lynda were snuggled beneath the covers on her bed. Her head was pillowed on his shoulder while her fingers absently drew meandering circles across his chest.

"You know, I had been wondering if the second time would be just as good as the first," she murmured drowsily. "Now I don't have to wonder. It was even better." She lifted her head just enough to give him a contented smile. "I'm so glad you could make it to town today. I don't think I could've made it much longer without being in your arms like this."

He placed a kiss on the top of her head. "I've been desperate to be with you again. This morning I was running around the ranch, doing chores as fast as I could so I could head over here."

And the minute he'd walked into the door, she'd flung herself into his arms and kissed him. One kiss was all it had taken for both of them to be sucked into a whirlwind of desire, and they'd left an urgent trail of clothing from the front door all the way to her bedroom. Now in the afterglow of their lovemaking, Gideon wondered how he'd managed to go without her for two hours, much less two days.

"I hope your father didn't need your help on the ranch this afternoon," she said.

"No. We managed to get it all done this morning. Dad promised to take Mom out this evening for dinner over in Bronco, so he wanted to get caught up on the heavy chores before I left."

"Hmm. What about Scotty? Did he want to come to town with you?"

"At first he was about to put up a loud howl. But then his grandparents told him they were taking him with them tonight, and he was one thrilled little boy."

"Do they often take Scotty with them? Or did they do it so you'd have the evening free?"

"They do take Scotty with them fairly often. But in this case, I think Dad guessed I was going to see you."

A slow smile tilted the corners of her lips. "So this means you don't have to hurry back."

With a growl of pleasure he stroked a hand down the middle of her bare back. "No hurrying. We're going to have a few private hours to ourselves."

Her hand moved from his chest to his arm where it slid all the way up to his shoulder, then down to his wrist. "Where did you get these muscles? Your arms and legs are like rocks."

With a grunt of humor, he said, "No special effort. Just riding horses. Lifting hay bales and feed sacks."

A chuckle rumbled her throat. "You mean you're not hung up on eating a pile of protein and running to the gym every chance you get?"

Grinning, he slid his hand over the indentation of her waist, then on to her hip. "I've never seen the inside of a gym, and I usually eat whatever I can scrounge up. Unless we're eating supper with my parents. So where did you get all these curves?"

"My mother. I was born with her curves."

"Lucky you. No, I should say lucky me." He shifted slightly in order to see her face. "Lynda, before we, uh, get carried away again there's something I wanted to ask you."

"Ask away."

"I wanted to see if you'd like to come to the ranch tomorrow afternoon. Scotty has been asking to see you."

"Has he? I wasn't quite sure what he thought about me. He gave me the impression that he liked me, but you never quite know what children are thinking."

"Your name comes out of his mouth every day. I think he's as smitten with you as I am."

"Aww. Well, I thought he was a pretty great little boy. But is he the only reason you want me to visit your ranch?" she asked.

"Hardly. I'd like to show you around the place. My house isn't exactly lavish, but it's very livable."

She let out a good-natured groan. "Oh, Gideon, I wouldn't care if you lived in a shack. I'm not into fancy or money."

"You dress fancy and you make plenty of money," he pointed out.

"Only because of my job. Otherwise you'd see me in jeans and a flannel shirt."

"And that is exactly what you should wear tomorrow. Will you come?"

Slipping her arm across his chest, she pulled herself

closer until half of her body was draped over his. "Yes, I will. I'm thrilled you asked me."

"Really?"

"Why do you sound surprised? It's not like you're asking me to marry you."

He tried not to stiffen at her offhand remark, but inside he was shaking as if he was standing in frigid wind without any clothes. Not because he was worried she was getting marriage on her mind. No. It was the exact opposite that was worrying him—because she'd never have marriage on her mind. And frankly, he didn't know how he was going to deal with the idea of a temporary relationship, or even if he should try.

Slipping his arm across her back, he shoved his dark thoughts aside. "Oh, I thought you being a city girl and all, you might not want to come out and slosh around the ranch yard."

"If I can slosh around with you and Scotty, it'll be great," she whispered.

Before he could make a reply, she covered his lips with hers, and that was all it took to send his hot desire for her roaring back to life.

The next afternoon as Lynda drove to Pine Ridge Ranch, she wasn't at all sure she should've accepted Gideon's invitation. And it had nothing to do with being in the countryside. She loved animals and the outdoors. She'd never minded getting her hands soiled or boots muddy. No, she was concerned that Gideon might make too much of her visit. After all, it was his home and with

Scotty present it would make the whole thing feel like a family gathering.

But when Gideon had extended the invitation to her, she'd not been able to refuse him. Actually, she'd felt a bit honored. Judging from a few remarks he'd made from time to time, he'd given her the impression he didn't invite women to his home. Perhaps because he didn't want to expose Scotty to any of his dates. Or could be he'd been gun shy after all he'd gone through with his ex-wife.

Thinking back, none of Lynda's boyfriends had invited her to their place just to show her around or visit with a family member. They'd only been interested in showing her the bed. Perry had promised to take her to his family home in Billings to meet his parents, but his promises had turned out to be as empty as a bucket with a hole in it. His reluctance to show her any sort of real commitment had slowly and surely hardened her.

But now with Gideon, she was feeling joy and a sense of belonging. Maybe where he was concerned, she wasn't exactly detached as she'd been with other men. But she felt certain she wasn't falling for him. No matter that Ruby thought she was getting serious about Gideon. Or that love wasn't something you put on a schedule like a dose of medication.

For today she was going to put her friend's words out of her mind. She wasn't going to let anything ruin her visit to Pine Ridge Ranch today.

Five minutes later, after she'd turned off the main road and bounced over a cattle guard at the entrance to the ranch, she passed a rambling L-shaped log house surrounded by a split-rail fence. Spruce trees dotted the front yard, and Lynda made a note to ask Gideon if his parents decorated the trees with Christmas lights. Having Scotty around probably gave the Frosts the initiative to celebrate the holidays in a big way.

A quarter mile on down from the main house, she turned onto a short gravel drive leading up to a smaller log house similar to the one she'd just passed. At one end a tall rock chimney puffed gray smoke. A mixture of pine, cedar, and hardwood trees grew in the front yard while a row of junipers sheltered the north side of the house. A gym set with a pair of swings and a slide sat beneath the bare branches of one of the hardwoods. To one side of that was a sandpile. A plastic dump truck and tractor was partially covered with the snow that had fallen two nights ago.

Scotty must have been watching for her. As soon as she parked her car behind Gideon's truck, the boy raced out the front door and down the steps to greet her.

When he reached her, Lynda knelt and gave him a tight hug. "Oh, I've been needing a hug like this. Thank you, Scotty."

"You're welcome," he said politely. "I've been needing a hug, too."

His reply was so like Gideon she had to smile. "Your house is very pretty. And I see you have a sandpile. Do you make little roads and caves and ponds?"

He grinned at her. "Yeah! How did you know?"

She gave him a wink. "Oh, I kinda know what little boys like. I have three nephews. The oldest, Bailey, is twelve, Ian is ten, and Cameron is eight. I bet you'd like to play with Cameron. He still likes to make roads and things, too."

"I'm gonna be eight someday when I get bigger. My birthday is October thirtieth."

She straightened to her full height. "Well now, that means you're a little spook or goblin on your birthday. Or are you a big orange pumpkin?" she teased.

Laughing, he grabbed her by the hand and tugged her in the direction of the house.

"That's silly," he said. "I'm not any of those things. I'm a cowboy like my dad."

He was also perfectly adorable like his dad, Lynda couldn't help thinking. "Of course," she told him. "Why didn't I know that? Maybe because you don't have on your cowboy boots today."

He giggled again. "I don't have 'em on 'cause Dad won't let me wear them in the snow. He says my feet will get wet and then I'll get sick."

"I think your dad is a smart man."

"Sure he is. He's a lawyer." He glanced curiously up at her. "Do you do what my dad does? Like go to court and argue?"

Lynda wanted to laugh, but somehow managed to keep a straight face. "I do. But we don't argue in court every day. That just happens on certain days."

As they approached a long, ground-level porch stretching the whole width of the house, the front door opened and Gideon stepped outside, wearing a green-plaid flannel shirt over a pair of faded jeans.

Smiling, he waved at them. "I see you have an escort," he called to Lynda.

She waved back at him. "Scotty is a great escort. He's keeping me steady on this snowy ground."

They walked onto the porch, and once she was standing at Gideon's side, he placed a tiny kiss on her cheek.

"I'm so glad you've come," he told her. Then, opening the door, he added, "Come on inside where it's warm."

The door opened directly into a living room furnished with a couch, two armchairs, and a love seat, all done in a combination of burgundy leather and wood. At one end, a fire was flaming high in the fireplace and in one corner a TV played a cartoon, but the volume was off.

"Let me take your coat, and I'll hang it up for you."

He helped her ease the heavy woolen coat off her shoulders, and as he carried it over to what she assumed was a coat closet, she said, "Thanks, but there's no need for you to take pains, Gideon. I wore old clothing today. Just in case we made a trek outdoors."

"Dad is cooking, Lynda," Scotty spoke up. "He wanted to make you something good to eat."

Surprised by this news, she looked over at Gideon to see he was scowling at his son.

"Scotty, you were supposed to keep that a secret."

The boy tilted his head from side to side in a defensive gesture. "Ah well, she was gonna figure it out sooner or later. And I didn't tell her what it was."

Lynda sniffed the air. "Whatever it is, it smells delicious."

"Oh, it's—"

"Scotty!" Gideon interrupted. "We can at least keep that a secret!"

Lynda affectionately scrubbed the top of Scotty's head. "Dad, you know it's hard to hold all that information inside," she teased.

"It's especially hard for Scotty," Gideon agreed. "Because he stuffs way too many things up there."

Taking her by the arm, he led her over to the love seat which was positioned in front of the fireplace. "Make yourself comfortable, and I'll get you something to drink."

"No. Don't bother. I'm fine. Just sit here with me," she told him. "And then I'd like to see the rest of your house. It's beautiful, Gideon. Did you help build it?"

Gideon sat down next to her, while Scotty sat cross-legged on the floor next to the fireplace.

"I did what I could. But I didn't have much time back then. I was still in college when the house was built. Cecily and I had just—" Pausing, he glanced over at Scotty, who was clearly all ears. "We were newlyweds then."

"In college studying law and a newlywed on top of that. How did you survive?"

He shrugged. "I had youth on my side. I can tell you I spent many a night burning the midnight oil over my books. But then, you went through it. You know what it takes to get through law school."

Strange, she thought, that both she and Gideon had gone through heartaches while they'd been working to become lawyers. It had been an especially difficult time for Lynda, but she figured what she'd gone through with

Perry didn't hold a candle to what Gideon had experienced with Cecily.

"Yes. Nothing about it was easy," she said, then smiled at him. "But look at us now. We're on easy street."

He chuckled, then his expression turned serious as he reached for her hand. "Yes, we're on easy street together."

Together. Hearing him say the word should have scared her. It was too intimate. Too indicative of the three of them as a family unit. It was a reminder that at one time she was 'together' with Perry, a union that had ended in disastrous fashion.

However, Lynda wasn't feeling anxious or trapped. So why wasn't she? Because sitting here with Gideon with his big warm hand wrapped around hers made her feel more special than she'd ever felt in her life?

She was probably turning into a gullible fool, she thought. But tonight she didn't want to let herself think of how painful it would be if Gideon decided she wasn't the right woman for him. Tonight she wasn't going to allow doubts and fears to chill the warm feelings inside her. She'd worry about getting hurt later.

Smiling, she squeezed his hand. "Yes. Together."

Chapter Nine

"Dad, I want to show Lynda my room first. I want her to see my dinosaur books. 'Cause she likes dinosaurs as much as I do."

Gideon chuckled as the three of them headed out of the living room. "You think so? Just because she helps out at the Dinosaur Center? I help out there, too, and I don't give a hoot about dinosaurs."

Scotty grabbed Lynda's hand and began leading her down a narrow hallway. "Dad, quit kiddin' us. You know you like dinosaurs. Even if you don't know as much about them as Lynda does."

Laughing, Lynda directed a wink over at Gideon. "If that's the case, Scotty, you and I have a lot to teach him."

"Yeah. He has a lot to learn before they start digging for bones."

Gideon said, "Speaking of digs. This past Friday at the Dinosaur Center, Krystal was in the snack room while I was in there getting a candy bar from the vending machine. She mentioned something about a strange guy showing up there earlier in the day. I meant to mention it to you, but then we, uh, got our mind on other things."

"Did she mention what he looked like?" Lynda asked.

"She said he was medium height—several inches shorter than me. He had dark hair and a distinctive gravelly voice. She was a little uneasy about him, because he kept prodding her for information about the dig. Like when it was scheduled to take place. The exact location and the company who'd be doing the excavating. None of those things have been decided yet. So it wasn't like she could give him any information."

Lynda paused for a thoughtful moment before she said, "It has to be Captain Hook. The unnerving pirate at the masquerade ball."

Frowning, Gideon said, "Didn't you say he was asking detailed questions about the dig that night?"

She nodded. "Yes. There's something weird going on with him, Gideon. Francine at the Silver Spur has been dealing with him coming into the restaurant and nosing around. I wouldn't be surprised if she didn't report him to the police."

"I'm beginning to think he might need to be reported."

"Dad! Lynda! Aren't you coming?"

Scotty's question caught their attention, and Lynda hurried forward to catch up to the boy. "Sorry, Scotty. Sometimes grown-ups forget what they're supposed to be doing," she told him.

He grinned at her. "It's okay. It's fun for you to be here. 'Cause I don't have a mommy. Well, I do have one—sort of. But she doesn't come here. I have to go see her. So she's not the same kind of mommies my friends have."

The child's words brought an ache to Lynda's heart,

and she instinctively wrapped an arm around his little shoulders and hugged him to her side. "I'm sure she loves you. And you know what? You have a really great dad, and he loves you lots. And I'm here with you now and I can't wait for you to show me your dinosaur books."

His eyes twinkled, and Lynda suddenly realized how much she wanted this child to be happy and to feel loved.

"Yeah! Just wait till you see how many I have!"

He took off in a run through the open doorway of his room, and Lynda paused long enough to glance back at Gideon. No doubt he'd heard what his son had said about his mother.

"Gideon, is it true that Cecily doesn't come out here to see Scotty?"

He grimaced. "It's true. And not because I'm against her visiting. She always hated being on the ranch. Now she says the place brings up too many bad memories. She'd rather visit Scotty on her turf."

"That's too bad."

His lips took on a rueful twist. "When I told you that Cecily was trying to be a better mother that's exactly what I meant. She's trying, but she still has a long way to go. I'm hoping that someday when she gets older and Scotty gets older, she'll realize the importance of being a committed mother. Until then—I'm trying to keep him happy and feeling loved."

The importance of being a committed mother. Strange how she'd heard those very same words before, but until this moment they'd not really stuck with her. Now she understood how much Scotty needed a mother on a permanent basis. He needed the reassurance that she would be there for him every day and night to love and comfort him. Just as Lynda's own mother had been there for her and her sisters.

Drawing in a deep breath, she squeezed his hand. "I'd better get in there and show Scotty how much I love dinosaurs. Lucky for me, the scary reptiles have created a bond between the two of us."

"I think even without the dinosaurs you and Scotty would click."

She smiled at him. "I'd like to think so, too."

She turned to head in the bedroom, then paused as Gideon whispered, "Thank you, Lynda."

"My pleasure. And thank you, Gideon, for letting me be a part of Scotty's life. I'm so glad he seems to like me. Because he's become a real joy to me."

Gideon had been far from certain how Lynda would react to his home and to Scotty's determination to monopolize her attention. But so far she'd praised everything about the house and had been extra gentle and understanding with Scotty. Actually, the rapport she had with his son gave him hope that she wasn't so resistant to having a family someday.

Eventually they bundled up and went outside for Lynda to get a look at the ranch yard. While they were looking over the fence at a pen full of calves, Scotty brought up the subject of the upcoming rodeo.

"Do you like rodeos, Lynda?"

Gideon couldn't help but notice Scotty had sidled up to Lynda and reached for her hand.

"I've only attended a few, but I enjoyed all of them," she told him. "Do you like going to the rodeo?"

"I like it a whole lot! I like to see all the bulls and horses buck the cowboys off," he added with a mischievous giggle. "Dad got bucked off last summer when a bee stung his horse. He could hardly walk after that."

Lynda directed a sly smile at Gideon before she turned her attention back to Scotty. "You mean your dad could hardly walk, or the horse?"

Her question produced a spate of giggles from Scotty. "The horse could walk good. Dad was limping around, but he got okay."

Gideon let out a good-natured groan. "You're not supposed to be telling Lynda such stories, son."

"But she likes them, Dad." He looked eagerly up at Lynda. "The Dinosaur Days Rodeo is going to be in Tenacity next month. And Geoff Burris is going to be there! He's a champion, and I really want to see him. Will you get a ticket and go with us, Lynda? I'd really like that."

She didn't answer immediately, and Gideon realized his son had put her on the spot. She wasn't ready to say she'd be around a month from now. Hell, he couldn't be sure she'd be around a week from now. She was unpredictable. And for reasons he didn't understand, she refused to commit herself to one special man or want love and marriage in her future. He knew all of this, and yet he couldn't send her out of his life. All he could do was hang on to to the hope that her attitude and her heart would change.

After a moment, she said, "Well, thank you for asking, Scotty. It sounds like fun, but next month is a long time from now. I'm not sure what I'll be doing then."

"Oh," he said glumly. "Maybe when the rodeo gets in town you'll know if you want to go."

Bending down, she gave him a hug. "If I do decide to go, Scotty, I promise it will be with you. Okay?"

The boy's face brightened considerably. "Okay!"

"Hey, Scotty? Want to go with us? We're going to throw hay out for the deer and elk."

Gideon looked around to see his parents had pulled up behind them in a work truck loaded down with several bales of alfalfa. Given the price of the hay, it was like throwing out gold coins, but his parents never failed to consider the winter plight of the wildlife.

With a hand at Lynda's back, he urged her away from the fence. "Come say hello to my parents," he told her.

Scotty raced ahead of them and climbed into the front seat between his grandparents, while Gideon and Lynda walked over to the driver's side where Ash had lowered the window.

"Dad, Mom, you remember Lynda Slater. She works with me at the firm," he said to his parents.

"Sure we do," Ash said with a friendly nod. "Nice to see you again, Ms. Slater."

"Oh, please call me Lynda," she said to him. "There's nothing formal about me."

On the opposite side of the truck cab, Joanne leaned over and gave Lynda a warm, welcoming smile. "I'm glad you could visit the ranch, Lynda. Have Gideon and Scotty been showing you around?"

"They've been giving me the grand tour. I'm enjoying seeing all the livestock. And Joanne, your chickens are beautiful," she said, then laughed. "Only there's one thing I haven't seen yet that Scotty keeps talking about. Bernie the bull. I hear he's in a far off pasture today."

Ash chuckled. "I imagine it would take a while to find Bernie today. Maybe he'll be closer to the ranch yard the next time you come for a visit," he told her.

"Has Gideon fed you yet?" Joanne asked as she cast a sly grin at her son. "He wouldn't let me fix you anything. So whatever he gives you is all his doing."

Lynda chuckled. "I'm not worried. Scotty has promised the food will be yummy."

Ash laughed. "What does my grandson know about food? He thinks licorice is yummy." He put the truck in gear and lifted a hand. "See you two later. We'll have Scotty back in an hour or so."

Scotty leaned his head up and looked out the window. "Will you be here when I get back, Lynda?"

Lynda gave the boy a little wave. "Of course I'll be here. I'd never leave without telling you goodbye first."

All smiles now, Scotty waved at them, then snuggled back against the seat as Ash slowly drove away. Once the truck moved out of sight, Gideon glanced down at Lynda.

"I wasn't expecting this to happen," he told her. "My parents must have decided we could use a little time to ourselves."

Grinning seductively, Lynda looped her arm through his. "A whole hour! You have some very thoughtful parents, Gideon."

"Come on," he said as he urged her toward the house. "Let's not waste any of this time they've handed us."

The next day at work, Lynda was straightening her desk as her lunch break approached. She was especially looking forward to lunch today because she and Gideon had invited Mary and John to join them at the Silver Spur. As long as the outing involved a group of staff members from Fiske and Jones, it was permissible. Still, she and Gideon had both promised to make a concentrated effort not to exchange any cheeky glances while they ate their meal.

As far as the rules of the law firm forbidding staff to date, Lynda didn't know yet what she and Gideon could do toward bending those restrictions. Neither of them should have to quit just because they wanted to be together. Hopefully, with a little luck and lawyering skills, they could persuade Aaron and Basil to abolish the silly rule.

And just why are you thinking that far ahead, Lynda? Remember, you're not falling in love. You're not making a commitment. Not to Gideon or any man.

The voice in her head caused her to pause and glance out the window. The weather had turned bright and beautiful today, and she wanted the rest of her day to be just as bright. She didn't want to worry about tomorrow or even the next day.

Will you get a ticket and go with us, Lynda? I'd really like that.

Scotty's sweet little voice was suddenly in her head, reminding her of the time she'd spent out at Pine Ridge Ranch. She'd not expected to like the place. She was a town girl, after all. But once she'd arrived on the ranch, she'd been awed by the beautiful countryside, and Gideon's comfortable log house had been the perfect image of a home. She'd even loved seeing the livestock and the work it involved to keep the animals healthy and sheltered. Most of all, though, she'd felt incredibly drawn to Scotty. And Gideon. Oh, Gideon. He made her heart skip and twirl. He made her float among the stars. She couldn't imagine her life without him.

She was mulling that thought over when she suddenly spotted the little dinosaur key ring she'd kept from the masquerade ball. Funny how the idea of finding the knight in shining armor seemed utterly ridiculous now. She had the thrill of Gideon's kisses, his arms to hold her tight. She hardly needed the mystery knight.

So your search for a good and honest man is over? You've decided you want Gideon in your life now and forever?

The questions darting through her head made her pause and think. Did she want a forever future with Gideon? Was he the man she wanted permanently by her side through life's ups and downs?

She glanced down at the key chain in her hand. The knight's kiss had been magical. But as Gideon had said, the knight was a fairy tale—just a brief moment in time. Gideon was real and different from any other man she'd ever known. Yes, she wanted to believe she'd found her forever prince charming in him.

A slight knock sounded on the door and she looked around to see Gideon step into the room. "Ready for lunch? John and Mary are waiting back in the locker room."

With a happy smile, she stepped toward him. "Here. Give this to Scotty. He might like to play with the little trinket or put it with his other dinosaur things."

He looked down at the key ring she placed in his hand and smiled sheepishly. "Oh, so you've finally figured out that he was me?"

It took a moment for his last word to sink in, and when it did, she was so completely stunned, she could only stare at him. Gideon was the mystery knight? The man who'd kissed her so passionately on the dance floor? The man she'd searched for and yearned to find?

Like a sudden bolt of lightning, hot anger flashed through her. "You! You were the knight at the ball?"

Surprise arched his brows. "Well, yes. I thought by now you'd probably figured out it was me. Isn't that why you gave me the key ring?"

"No! I hadn't figured it out!" she practically yelled at him. "I didn't know until now—this very second. And you let me go around asking all over town about the unknown man in a knight costume! You didn't care that I was making an utter fool of myself. Now everyone is probably thinking I'm the biggest chump in Tenacity!"

He let out a rueful groan. "Lynda, the folks around here aren't thinking anything of the sort. According to you, none of the people you asked knew I was the knight. So there. You have nothing to be embarrassed about."

"But I know! Why didn't you tell me before? Or were you never planning to tell me?"

Not waiting to hear his reply, she pulled on her coat and snatched her purse off the corner of the desk and stormed out of the office. He followed directly on her heels.

"You don't understand, Lynda. The day after the ball, I was shocked when you started talking about your mystery knight. That night—when I walked up to you at the ball and we began dancing I expected you to recognize me. And then later, well, I thought by now you'd probably figured out that I was the knight in shining armor. And then when we kissed, I was certain you'd guessed it was me."

"Oh sure. Since we'd kissed so much before that night, it was a cinch I would guess your identity!" she practically yelled at him. "You're a lying jerk, Gideon Frost!"

"I didn't lie to you," he argued. "I just didn't tell you the whole truth!"

She glared at him. "You sound just like a damned lawyer," she said through gritted teeth.

His arms lifted and fell in a helpless gesture. "I am a lawyer. Should I apologize for that, too?"

"Apologies won't do you any good. It's too late for those now!" She started down the hallway and noticed some of the staff members were leaning out their doors, staring to see what the loud voices were about. Lynda didn't care what they'd heard or that they'd just revealed to the whole office that they'd been a couple. She was beyond caring about anything except running from the pain in her heart.

He hurried after her. "Lynda, if you'll calm down and think this through, you'll realize the kiss we shared at the masquerade ball is definite proof we belong together. Or was chasing a fairy tale all you've ever been interested in?"

"Hardly! And you've given me definite proof I don't really know who you are. But there's one definite thing I do know—I need space from you!"

She stalked off and didn't stop until she was outside, climbing behind the steering wheel of her car. And by then angry tears were streaming down her face.

Two days later, Gideon was standing at the gas range in his kitchen, frying bacon in an iron skillet while asking himself for the umpteenth time what, if anything, he could do to make things right between him and Lynda.

In her eyes, he supposed he did look guilty of lies and deceit. But he'd not kept the identity of the knight a secret as a way to hurt her. He'd always planned to tell Lynda that he was the knight in shining armor. But the situation had barreled out of control before he could say anything to her. That next morning after the ball, she'd been so wound up in telling their friends all about the kiss, he'd not wanted to confess he was the knight and embarrass her in front of them. And then later, the more he thought about it, the more he was afraid it might ruin their friendship and the fragile relationship that was building between them. So he'd decided to wait until their relationship was more solid and he could explain things in a gentle way, at the right time. But when she'd handed him the dinosaur key chain, he'd felt certain she was admitting she'd already guessed he was her mystery man. Now she thought he'd been a deceptive jerk and wasn't speaking to him. And he had no idea if she'd ever find it in her heart to forgive him.

The kitchen door leading onto the back porch opened, and he turned away from the range to see Scotty walking through the door carrying a small basket of eggs.

"I see you have eggs with you. Grandma's hens must've decided to start laying."

The boy walked over to the cabinet and placed the basket next to the sink. "Grandma said she has plenty of eggs right now, so she said to give these to you. She let me help her clean out the nesting boxes, and we put new straw and hay for the hens to sit on."

Normally, when Scotty helped one or both of his grandparents with an important chore, he always came running back into the house all excited. However, this evening there wasn't so much as a smile on his face. Gideon didn't know exactly what was causing the boy to seem subdued. He'd not told him about his breakup with Lynda, but he was beginning to suspect the boy had somehow sensed something was not right with his father.

"I'm glad you helped her, Scotty. You're a good boy."

"Am I good, Dad?"

Gideon switched off the burner beneath the sizzling bacon and turned to look at his son. "Why would you ask me such a thing, Scotty? Of course you're a good boy. Have you done something wrong that you haven't told me about?"

Scotty glumly shook his head. "No. But why hasn't Lynda come back to see us? She said she'd come back real soon. But you said she might not come see us for a long time. She must've thought I was bad. 'Cause that's why my mommy never came back. She said I always misbehaved."

"Oh, son, no!" Quickly squatting to Scotty's level, Gideon gathered both of his little hands between his. "Did your mommy really tell you such a thing?"

"Well, not exactly. She said I was naughty sometimes. So I thought that's why she didn't come see us." A glum frown drooped the corners of his mouth. "And now Lynda don't want to see us anymore."

"Where did you get that idea?"

"Well, 'cause you haven't been talking about her or saying she was coming out here to see us."

The forlorn sound in Scotty's voice literally broke Gideon's heart. It also made him feel very guilty and angry at himself. Scotty had already suffered too much loss and disruption in his life. He didn't need another woman coming along and showing him affection, then jerking it all away.

Gideon should've been putting his son's happiness before his own selfish need for Lynda. He should've never kissed her, and he sure as hell shouldn't have fallen into bed with her. He was an adult; he'd somehow manage to deal with their breakup. But how could a four-year-old little boy understand? And neither did the boy deserve it, he thought angrily.

Hugging Scotty to him, he gently rubbed his back. "Listen, Scotty, you're the best little boy anybody could ever have. I love you more than anything, and I'm proud of you. And no matter what, we'll always be together. That will never change." He eased the child out of his arms, then lifted his chin so he could look him square in the eyes. "As for Lynda, don't be worrying about her. She's a very busy lady. It may take her a while to come see you again."

A light of hope flickered in the boy's brown eyes. "Do you think she liked me, Dad?"

Gideon gave him a bright smile. "Sure, she did. She kissed you when she left, didn't she?"

Grinning now, Scotty rubbed his cheek. "Yeah, she did. And you know what, Dad? I still believe Lynda will decide to go to the rodeo with us. And one of these days she's gonna be my mommy."

There was as much a chance of that happening as a flying saucer landing in the front yard, but he wasn't going to burst Scotty's bubble. For right now the boy had hope. And Gideon was trying to hold on to the last shred of hope he possessed.

"Where did you get that idea, son? Did Lynda say anything about being your mommy?"

Scotty shook his head. "No. But I just know, 'cause—well, I just know."

Gideon had no idea where Scotty had gotten such a strong conviction about Lynda becoming his mother. And he wasn't going to press the child about the matter. He only prayed that his son's heart wouldn't eventually be broken, the way Gideon's was breaking now.

A week later, Lynda was wondering if she was coming down with a virus or some sort of late-winter flu bug. At least that was what she was asking herself as she drove down Central Avenue on her way home from work. There was no way she was feeling this drained and empty because she and Gideon had parted ways. No, a person had to be in love before their heart could be broken, and hers was beating just fine. She just needed to get back on track to being Lynda Slater, the free spirit, then the world would look right again. And she'd *feel* right again.

And the best way to get back on track was to go out. Staying home was just making her more miserable.

Since that day he'd admitted to being the knight, they'd not spoken, except for a few necessary words they'd exchanged while working at the Dinosaur Center. Their volunteer work together had become nearly unbearable for Lynda. Sitting next to him for two hours, drawing in his masculine scent, watching the muscles in his long legs strain against his jeans and the fabric of his shirt stretch across the back of his broad shoulders. Everything about him made her ache with longing, but she doggedly resisted touching him, much less talking to him.

The driveway into Grizzly Bar's parking lot appeared up ahead and she flipped on her blinker to make the turn, but at the last second, she turned it off and steered the car down the street.

Who the hell was she kidding? The mere idea of sitting on a hard bar stool and making small talk to Dale Clutterbuck left her cold. The experience wouldn't be an enjoyment; it would be torture. Nothing like the easy conversation she had with Gideon or the warm laughter they shared. He was the one she wanted to be with… So what did that mean for her future? That she'd ruined everything? That her joy for life had vanished when she ended her chance with Gideon?

Groaning miserably, she made a U-turn at the next intersection and headed the car toward Vanessa's place. If anyone could reason out a problem, it was her older sister.

When Lynda parked her car in the driveway and walked up to the door, she could hear kids yelling over the roar of a vacuum cleaner. Doubtful the sound of her knock would be heard, she started to punch the doorbell, but before she could reach the button, the door popped open and her brother-in-law, Gage, stepped out.

"Lynda! What are you doing standing out here? No need to knock—that bunch will never hear you anyway." Chuckling, he gave her a hug. "Sorry I can't stick around. A company meeting tonight."

"We'll visit another time, Gage."

He jerked his thumb back toward the house as he started down the steps. "See if you can quiet things down in there before the neighbors call the police."

Normally Lynda would be laughing, but she had to force a chuckle. "I'll try."

Gage went on his way, and Lynda entered the house. Vanessa wasn't in the living room, but all three of her nephews were banging each other with throw pillows while little Martha was attempting to push the vacuum over a large area rug. Trail mix was scattered across the plush rug and over the hardwood floor.

The second the kids spotted her entering the room, they all rushed to give their aunt a hug.

"What's going on in here?" Lynda demanded. "Why

are you boys roughhousing while your sister is doing the cleaning?"

"Ian and Cameron made the mess," Bailey, the eldest, blurted out.

Martha jammed a hand on her hip and stated in an indignant voice, "I'm vacuuming 'cause my brothers can't do it right. And Mother said every crumb better be up, or we won't get to go to the basketball game Friday night."

"Yeah. And me and Martha didn't even make the mess!" Bailey complained.

Lynda patted the top of his head, a feat that was becoming harder since the boy had already surpassed her height. "Goes to show you that being in the wrong company can get you in trouble."

"Are you going to eat with us, Aunt Lynda?" Cameron asked. "We get to eat junk food tonight."

"Junk food?" Lynda asked. "Your mother must be slipping."

"Dad won't be here to eat, so we're getting takeout," Ian explained. "Chicken nuggets and corndogs. Mm-mmm."

"And french fries," Martha added.

"Sounds yummy," Lynda agreed with as much enthusiasm as she could muster. "Where's your mother? In the kitchen?"

Martha said, "She went to her bedroom to change and hasn't come out yet."

"She might have gone to bed. I think her head was hurting," Ian declared.

Bailey gave his younger brother a hard whack with

the throw pillow. "You two goons would make anybody's head hurt!"

Lynda held up a hand. "Time-out! Or I'm going to make you all eat canned tuna and crackers for supper."

Thankfully, the kids went quiet, and Lynda left the living room before more chaos broke out.

When she knocked on Vanessa's bedroom door, her sister yelled out, "I'm changing! And don't go in the kitchen until I come out!"

"Van, it's me, Lynda."

The door jerked open and her frazzled-looking sister jerked her into the cluttered bedroom. "Lynda! When did you get here?"

"Only a few minutes ago. I met Gage on the way in."

Vanessa dug a T-shirt from a drawer and pulled it over her head. "A quarterly meeting. He hates them, but they're necessary. So what are you doing this evening?"

"Nothing. I was on my way home from the office and started to go to Grizzly's for happy hour, but—"

"You weren't feeling so happy, right?" she asked as she stepped into a pair of baggy jeans.

"How did you guess?"

"Your face. You look like the judge just ruled against you."

Sighing, Lynda brushed aside a pile of clothing on a dressing bench and sat down. "It's much worse than losing a court case. I've messed up royally."

Vanessa stepped around the corner of the bed to stand in front of her. "How? What's happened?"

She drew in a deep breath, then blurted the words

out before she could stop them. "I—I think I've fallen in love."

Her sister's eyes widened, and Lynda knew the revelation had given Vanessa a much harder whack than Bailey had given his brother with the throw pillow.

"I'm floored! My sister, Lynda, saying the *L*-word!"

"I know. It sounds crazy. But I don't know how else to describe this…thing that's come over me."

Frowning, Vanessa's head moved slowly from side to side. "I don't understand. You just said you messed up. If you've fallen in love, I wouldn't call that messing up. I'd call that a hallelujah-finally thing."

"I suppose it could've been a hallelujah thing if I hadn't thrown a fit. Not that it wasn't justified. But truth be told, I think I was beginning to ruin things even before my tantrum."

The frown on Vanessa's face deepened. "I think you'd better start at the beginning. First of all who is this man you've fallen in love with?"

Lynda looked hopelessly at her sister. "You're not going to believe this, but I found my knight in shining armor. The one who kissed me at the masquerade ball and turned me into some sort of romantic idiot."

"Just a minute. I need to sit down for this." She pulled up a footstool and took a seat directly in front of Lynda. "Okay. You honestly found your knight? When? Why didn't you tell your sisters about this already?"

Grimacing, Lynda said, "Because I didn't know the man I was falling in love with was the knight. Not until he admitted it about a week and a half ago. That's when

I blew my lid. I was so angry that he'd made me look like a fool!"

"How did he do that? Was he stringing you along like Perry?"

Lynda couldn't hold her sister's gaze. "No. He's nothing like Perry. He wasn't stringing me along. He's actually a very wonderful man—a family man, raising his four-year-old son."

"Does this man live here in Tenacity?"

"Not here in town. He lives on his family's ranch some distance north of town. He, uh—it's Gideon Frost. He's a fellow lawyer at Fiske and Jones, and he also helps his parents run the family ranch."

"Gideon Frost—yes! I remember meeting him at that Fiske and Jones party. He's a good-looking young guy, but I'd never imagined you two together! You with a father. A responsible family man. What made you go for him?"

What had made her fall for Gideon, she asked herself. "I don't know exactly. We'd worked around each other for more than two years. But I'd never noticed him. He's six years younger than me, and I always had this impression that he was a stuffed shirt and too strait laced for me. Boy, was I ever wrong about that. But Van, with Gideon it turned out to be much more than sex. I can't explain or describe the feelings he's brought out of me. And now… I was so angry about the knight thing that I yelled at him and told him I needed space. He hasn't spoken to me since."

"I don't blame him. Sorry, sis, I know you're a lawyer and you're supposed to know how to consult and negotiate, but it sounds like you did a miserable job with your Gideon."

Her Gideon. If only he was *her* Gideon, she thought. "Okay, I admit I did everything wrong. But I was so shocked—he should have confessed right from the start that he was the knight. Instead, he let me ask all over town if anyone knew the knight. He said he didn't say anything because he thought I'd already suspected it was him. And that it really didn't matter."

"It shouldn't matter. If you love the guy, Lynda, you can't let a thing like this stand in your way."

"He wasn't truthful with me!"

"Over a silly masquerade costume? Come on! Why don't you admit that the real reason you're so worked up over Gideon is because he's broken through those thick walls you've had around you for all these years."

Lynda groaned. "My heart is tough," she muttered. "No man is going to break through it. And that includes, Gideon."

"Hah!" Vanessa snorted. "You're the one who's lying now. You're not angry and miserable because this guy turned out to be the knight. You're running scared because you love him, and you're running scared. You're afraid of losing your independence and leaning on a man. Even more, you're afraid Gideon might turn out to be deceptive like Perry and hurt you. Lynda, Gideon's secret about being the white knight can't be compared to Perry's lies about loving you and marrying you. There's a world of difference."

"Yes, okay, I can admit Gideon's fib is forgivable," she said, then, with a heavy sigh, thrust a hand through her hair. "And I guess ever since my law school days I have been afraid of being hurt again. But that's only a part of my concerns, Van. I've been a free bird for a long time, and believed I always would be. But now—everything feels different. Do you know what I was thinking when I walked into this house a few minutes ago and found your kids fighting?"

"Probably that I'm not doing a very good job of mothering," Vanessa said wryly.

"No. You're a wonderful mother, Van. What instantly came to my mind was little Scotty—Gideon's son. He needs brothers and sisters like your children have. Like you and I have. He doesn't know what a special joy it is to have a sibling. He doesn't even know what it's like to have a full-time mother. He only sees her every other weekend."

Vanessa reached for Lynda's hand and squeezed it tightly. "Sounds like you've fallen in love with Scotty, too."

Tears stung the back of Lynda's eyes as she thought of how the boy had asked her to go to the rodeo with him and his dad and she'd put him off. She'd been afraid to say she'd be with Gideon and him a month from now or even a week from now. She'd been so wrong. So wrong.

"Van, I've never thought of myself as a wife or mother. Can I be those things for him and Scotty and do them right? Especially in Gideon's eyes."

"If he truly loves you then he's going to see you just as you are now—a kind and loving woman, who's doing the best she can for her family. The same way I see the man I love when I look at Gage. It will be the same way with you and Gideon—if you let it."

If she'd let it.

She was willing to try. But what about Gideon? Would he understand why she'd been so hesitant up to now about making a commitment to him and Scotty? Did he care enough about her to want to make a future with her? He'd never said the word love to her. But maybe that was because he'd needed to hear it from her first.

She could only hope.

The next evening, Gideon was sitting in front of the fireplace, trying to concentrate on a brief he'd written for a case he'd be dealing with in the next few days, when Scotty looked up from playing on the floor. "You know what Grandma told me when I was helping her wash the dishes tonight?"

For the past half hour, the boy had been quiet as he'd built a house and fence out of his Lincoln Logs, but now Gideon could tell something had been going around in his son's thoughts.

"No. That she wants a bigger chicken house before spring gets here?"

"Yeah. She told me that. But something else, too. She says her and Grandpa are going to go see Geoff Burris at the Dinosaur Days Rodeo."

Gideon tried not to stiffen at the mention of the rodeo. He knew how much it had disappointed Scotty when Lynda had put him off on the subject of going.

Damn it! He wished to hell he could quit thinking about her. But try as he might, he couldn't think of anything except how much he missed her, how much he wanted her in his and Scotty's life. Was he crazy for wanting a free-spirited woman like Lynda? Was he a glutton for punishment? Because the way things looked now, misery was all he was going to get from her.

Today when they were doing their charity work at the Dinosaur Center, he'd wanted to ask her if she was really over him. He wanted her to tell him straight out whether they had a chance of finding lasting happiness together. But she'd remained stubbornly quiet the whole time they'd been there, and several times he'd caught her looking at him in an odd way. And in the end, he'd decided not to say anything. She was clearly over him, and he could simply count himself as nothing more than a notch on her bedpost.

"Dad, did you hear me?"

"I heard you, son. Did Grandma ask if you wanted to go to the rodeo with them?"

"Yes. But I told her we'd be going with Lynda."

Gideon put the brief aside and looked directly at Scotty. "Son, why did you tell her such a thing? You don't know for certain that you'll be going to the rodeo with Lynda. And right now she's kind of unhappy with me."

He could have told Scotty he doubted they'd be seeing her any time soon. Or maybe never, Gideon thought. But he didn't want to be that blunt and brutal with Scotty right now. The child shouldn't have to hurt because of Gideon's misjudgment in women. And from now on, he was going to make sure it never happened again. Even if it meant he remained a bachelor for the rest of his life.

"I know she's unhappy," Scotty said.

"And how would you know such a thing?"

"Well, I can tell. Because you've been sad."

Gideon sighed. "Look, son, I don't want you worrying about any of this. You and I—we're going to be just fine. Understand?"

"Sure, Dad. And Lynda will be fine, too. You just wait and see."

Biting back a sigh, Gideon wiped a hand over his face. Perhaps it was a good thing Scotty had such a positive outlook. It was far better than seeing the boy in tears.

"You sound pretty confident."

He gave his father an emphatic nod. "That's 'cause Winona told me so."

Frowning now, Gideon scooted to the edge of the couch to peer earnestly at his son. "Are you talking about Winona—a really old woman?"

Scotty nodded. "She looks real old, but she didn't act old. She came by school one day and was talking to Miss Renegar about something out in the hall."

"So how did you happen to talk to Winona?"

"The bell rang and it was time for my class to go to lunch. She caught me when I passed by her. She took hold of my hand and looked me in the eyes—it was kinda scary. 'Cause her hand was really bony and wrinkly, and she was dressed kinda funny. But I didn't want to be rude, so I stood there. That's when she told me her name and that I was going to get a full-time mommy real soon. And then she patted my cheek and let me go."

Incredulous, Gideon asked, "And you believed her?"

Scotty nodded emphatically. "Yeah. After she held

my hand I wasn't scared no more. I felt good 'cause I could tell she wanted me to be happy."

Gideon's mind was whirling. Winona. Winona Cobbs-Sanchez! The mystic woman Lynda had talked about asking for help to find the mystery knight. Lynda had said Winona was all about trying to help people. But never would Gideon have dreamed Scotty would cross paths with the physic! How the hell was Gideon going to explain to his son that Winona didn't know what she was talking about and Lynda was well and truly out of their lives?

"I see. So why haven't you told me about Winona before now?"

Scotty pursed his lips together. "Because you wouldn't have believed me. Just like you don't believe Lynda will go to the rodeo with us."

Gideon was wondering how he could argue Scotty's point when the doorbell suddenly broke the silence.

"I'll answer it!" Scotty cried out.

The boy took off in a run to the door, and Gideon yelled at him, "Wait a minute. You know you're not to open the door unless you know who it is!"

Scotty peeped through a window at the side of the door, then jumped joyously up and down. "It's Lynda!"

Lynda?

Gideon quickly unlocked the door and pulled it open, but Scotty didn't give him a chance to invite her inside. The boy threw himself straight at her and wrapped his little arms around her legs. "Lynda! You came! I knew you would! I knew it!"

Smiling, she bent down and lifted Scotty into her arms. "How's my little cowboy?"

As she pecked a kiss on his cheek, Gideon didn't miss the glaze of tears in her eyes. Was he seeing things? He couldn't quite believe she was here.

"I'm really good," Scotty said, his face beaming. "And I'm happy to see you."

"I'm happy to see you, too, Scotty." She set the boy back on his feet before she turned to Gideon. "Am I interrupting? I started to call, but I was… I didn't want to give you the chance to tell me to stay away."

He finally managed to breathe even though the sight of her had whammed him straight in the middle of his chest. "You're not interrupting. But I think—" He glanced at Scotty's smug little face. "I need to take Scotty over to his grandparents so the two of us can talk."

After ordering Scotty to grab his coat, he turned to Lynda and motioned to the love seat in front of the fireplace. "Make yourself comfortable. I'll be back in a couple of minutes."

Once Gideon left with Scotty, she walked over to the love seat, but she was too nervous to sit. Instead, she stood by the hearth and stretched out her hands toward the warmth of the flames.

All day long at work, she'd been trying to think of the most convincing words she could say to him. And on her way over here, she'd tried to decide the best way to explain her behavior. Not just about the masquerade ball and the knight, but during the whole time they'd been together. She was a lawyer, and she'd been praised for being able to use just the right words at the right time in the courtroom. But this wasn't a courthouse. And she wasn't dealing with a judge. This was the man she loved.

The sound of the door opening and closing had her turning away from the fire, and a lump of emotion filled her throat as she watched him remove his coat, then cross the room to stand in front of her.

"I'm not going to waste your time or mine with small talk," he said. "I'll just come straight out with it. Why are you here? We were alone together at the Dinosaur Center this afternoon. You could've talked to me then. Actually, you've had plenty of days to talk to me, but you haven't. Why now? Tonight? Why draw Scotty into it? Don't you think you've hurt my child enough?"

"I understand you're furious with me. I don't blame you. And I didn't say anything this afternoon, because—well, the Dinosaur Center wasn't the time or place for such a conversation."

His features were as hard as granite, and Lynda hated herself for causing him such anger and pain.

"And just what kind of conversation were you planning to have with me? You want to remind me that I'm a big liar and letting you go on believing in the knight was wrong of me. Well, I guess it was wrong of me. I guess I was a big coward for not telling you the truth the very next day. But just in case you're interested, I was knocked for a loop over our kiss that night at the ball. And I knew if I told you I was the knight, the chance for us to ever get together would be over."

"Oh, Gideon," she whispered, her voice stricken with regret. "I've been so wrong. Wrong about everything. I think—this thing between us is like nothing I'd ever felt before and I think I went a little crazy. My sister said I've been running scared. And she's right. I have been running scared from the idea of marriage and motherhood and being worthy of the woman you and Scotty need and deserve in your life."

His stony features softened as he stepped forward and wrapped his hands around her upper arms. "Just what are you feeling for me, Lynda? If it's just torrid sex you're wanting, then we need to end this thing once and for all."

She placed her hands on his chest, and the beat of his heart beneath her palm felt so precious it very nearly brought tears to her eyes. "I should have told you days ago that I love you. I think I fell in love with you that first day we got together. I hope it's not too late for us to start over. Seriously start over."

He pulled her to him and rested his cheek against the top of her head. "I love you, Lynda. I think I've loved you since the moment I laid eyes on you. But I have Scotty to consider. I can't let him be hurt if you decide you're not serious about being in our lives."

"I understand. And you should feel that way. But I'm telling you that I am serious. I am sure. I want us to be together from now on—for the rest of our lives."

He eased her back from him, and his eyes were full of wonder as they searched her face. "You really mean that?"

Smiling now, she reached in her pocket and pulled out a velvet box. When she opened it, the glow from the firelight winked over a pair of matching gold wedding bands.

"This is how much I mean it, Gideon. Will you marry me? Will you let me be your wife and the mother of your children?"

"Children? As in plural?"

She laughed. "I happen to think Scotty needs some siblings. Don't you?"

Groaning with joy, he placed a long, sweet kiss on her lips. "Yes to the children. Yes to being your husband. I'll marry you as soon as we can get a wedding planned."

"Are you sure?" she asked coyly.

He laughed under his breath. "Sorry, sweetheart—you're never going to get rid of me now. Come on, let's go get Scotty and give him the news."

Five minutes later, in front of the main ranch house, Gideon honked the horn, and Scotty came racing out to join them.

Since they were only going a quarter of a mile on a private road, Gideon allowed the boy to sit between him and Lynda in the front seat.

"So are you guys happy together now?" he asked as his gaze swung back and forth between the two adults.

Lynda laughed, and with her arm around his little shoulders, she hugged him close to her side. "We are very happy together. We're going to get married. And I'm going to be your step- mom. That is, if you want me to be," she added.

His face was a picture of wonder as he looked from her to his father. "Dad, is she telling me the truth? Are you getting married?"

Grinning, Gideon said, "We are. So Winona turned out to be right after all."

With a comical frown, Lynda looked over at him. "What's this? Are you talking about Winona Cobbs-Sanchez?"

Gideon nodded. "I didn't hear about this until tonight, but my son—our son, now—had a chance meeting with her some time back. She predicted he was going to meet someone soon who would hold his hand like his dad."

"Oooh! And now he is getting one! The future must have been written in the stars, and Winona read it."

He cast her a tender look. "The stars must have been shining down on us at the masquerade ball, too."

"And they'll never stop shining down on us," she murmured to Gideon, then ruffled the top of Scotty's hair. "Guess what, cowboy, I have three tickets to the Dinosaur Days Rodeo. Think you'll be ready to see Geoff Burris and all those bucking bulls and broncos?"

"Yippee! I'll be more than ready!"

Much later that night, long after Scotty had fallen asleep, Gideon and Lynda were snuggled together in his big four-poster bed. Only moments before, he'd been soaring through a velvet black sky with Lynda wrapped so tightly in his arms they moved as one body and one heart, floating and swirling straight to the moon. And now, as he stroked a hand over her hair, then onto the mound of one breast, he could only think how perfectly right it was for her to be at his side, her cheek resting against the rapid beat of his heart.

Outside the windows of the bedroom, a cold wind was shaking the limbs of the junipers and sweeping across the ranch yard, but Gideon was certain he'd never have another cold night. Not with Lynda warming him inside and out.

"Happy?" she asked.

"I didn't know feeling like this was possible," he admitted. "I never thought…after everything I went through I doubted I could ever feel much of anything. I was numb for a long time—until you."

Her hand softly caressed his arm. "Oh, Gideon, I'm going to make sure you and Scotty are never hurt again."

Rolling onto his side, he gently cupped his hand to the side of her face. "Now that we're in a good place, there's something I need to know. All these years you made a point of avoiding any kind of serious commitment to marriage or a family. I often heard you say that family life wasn't for you. Why?"

"It's not some deep dark secret, Gideon. It's just a hard fact that I carried around for far too long. You see, when I was in law school I fell for a med student. And to make a long story short, he strung me along with empty promises until he finally gave me the brush-off—as if I meant nothing. After that something in me turned hard. I was determined to never let another man use me or let my feelings get involved. And I didn't—until you kissed me at the ball."

"But you didn't know it was me," he interrupted.

She touched a forefinger to his lips. "True. It's funny but when we kissed at the library it was like a light flashed on and I wondered why you tasted like the knight. I should have known."

He chuckled under his breath. "I was having all kinds of flashes that day."

She tilted her head just enough to press a kiss to his chin. "Now that we know where we've both been and where we're going, we still have a little problem."

He meshed his fingers in her hair and massaged the tips against her scalp. "I know. Fiske and Jones. How are we going to convince our bosses they need us even though we'll be husband and wife?"

"Hmm. We both have an excellent track record with the firm. And I believe I'm a fairly good persuader. I feel certain I can convince Aaron and Basil that they need us. Plus, convince them they need to abolish the fraternizing rule. Especially in a town the size of Tenacity."

With a groan of pleasure, he pressed a hand against the small of her back and rolled her closer to his side. "I'm good at persuading, too. Think I can persuade you to do a little more fraternizing with me again tonight?"

"I'm convinced," she whispered against his lips.

He started to kiss her, then abruptly lifted his head. "I forgot. I used my last condom."

A clever smile spread across her lovely face. "We don't need one, Gideon. I'm thirty-three and Scotty is four. It's time we start working on expanding the Frost family. Don't you think?"

His heart overflowing, he brought his lips next to hers. "I couldn't agree more, my darling Lynda."

* * * * *